INSIDE BURN

Praise for *The Sound of Water*

'[An] amazing novel that combines poetry and spirituality, narrative verve and environmental complaint.'

—*Panorama Magazine*

'Revealing, moving and well-written debut offers a dramatic, engaging lens through which to view an endlessly complex country.'

—**Kirkus Review**

'This book should be made required reading for every bureaucrat, politician and schoolchild in this country.'

—*India Today*

'A great debut novel that transcends the limits of storytelling and in doing so transforms into an archetype of life itself.'

—*The Tribune*

Praise for *Hul: Cry Rebel*

'Sanjay Bahadur takes his novel to a riveting climax.'

—*Nepali Times*

'This is a novel worth reading more than once.'

—**Dame Greta Rana**, *Pan Asia*

'A must-read for war-torn people.'

—*The Himalayan Times*

'Powerful and moving.'
—**Pritish Nandy**

'A real page-turner.'
—*Outlook*

'Captivating and the plot rigorously researched … a deserving climax.'
—*The Hindustan Times*

'A marvellous storyteller, among the best.'
—**Mani Shankar Aiyar**, *Mail Today*

'An engaging historical novel.'
—*DNA*

Praise for *Bite of the Black Dogs*

'Bahadur is someone on a quest to write across genres.'
—*The Hindustan Times*

'The book, which comes at a time of grim attrition in the Valley, sets new standards for candid narratives about the soldiers who inhabit our shadowlands.'
—*The Hindu*

'All in all, the book is a moving record of real-time handling of the situation by the armed forces today in Jammu and Kashmir.'
—*Deccan Chronicle*

'Bahadur manages, in vivid detail and with admirable accuracy, to take us through the lives of the various actors in his tale, from the insurgents trained across the border to the people of the Valley, and, of course, the armed forces.'

—*The Indian Express*

'[An] unputdownable read where the reader can vividly witness the actions unfolding right in front of their eyes.'

—**Millenium Post**

'The build-up is excellent, racy and so is the climax—you can hear, feel and see the gunshots, the gory hand-to-hand struggles, the explosions, and the rain-lashed, precariously narrow mountain paths that the militants and the Special Forces pound across on foot.'

—*Deccan Herald*

INSIDE BURN

A Novel

SANJAY BAHADUR

Harper
Fiction

An Imprint of HarperCollins Publishers

First published in India by Harper Fiction 2024
An imprint of HarperCollins *Publishers*
4th Floor, Tower A, Building No. 10, DLF Cyber City,
DLF Phase II, Gurugram, Haryana – 122002
www.harpercollins.co.in

2 4 6 8 10 9 7 5 3 1

Copyright © Sanjay Bahadur 2024

P-ISBN: 978-93-6213-334-2
E-ISBN: 978-93-6213-662-6

This is a work of fiction and all characters and incidents described in this book are the product of the author's imagination. Any resemblance to actual persons, living or dead, is entirely coincidental.

Sanjay Bahadur asserts the moral right
to be identified as the author of this work.

All rights reserved. No part of this publication may be reproduced, stored in a retrieval system, or transmitted, in any form or by any means, electronic, mechanical, photocopying, recording or otherwise, without the prior permission of the publishers.

Typeset in 11.5/14.2 Adobe Garamond at
Manipal Technologies Limited, Manipal

Printed and bound at
Thomson Press (India) Ltd

*To my mother, Bimla Bahadur (1936–2019),
who taught me my first words*

Broken windows theory: academic theory proposed by James Q. Wilson and George Kelling in 1982 that used broken windows as a metaphor for disorder within neighbourhoods. Their theory links disorder and incivility within a community to subsequent occurrences of serious crime.

Mumbai rail commuters go on rampage to protest delay

The violent protests led to the complete disruption of train services for more than seven hours.

MUMBAI | JANUARY 02, 2015

Enraged commuters went on the rampage, upset over the delay in suburban local train services on the central line which carries half of Mumbai's rail passengers, bringing the city's lifeline to a complete halt.

It all started during the peak hours on Friday morning after a pantograph of one of the local trains was broken near Thakurli station on up slow line. Tempers flared as hundreds of commuters found themselves stranded at Diva Junction station.

The mob pelted stones at the trains, vandalized railway property and torched three vehicles including a police van at Diva Junction railway station on Central Railway, on the outskirts of Mumbai.

https://timesofindia.indiatimes.com/city/mumbai/mumbais-lifeline-snaps-as-irate-commuters-run-riot/articleshow/45736502.cms

Violence rocks Jaipur, 1 dies

JAIPUR | SEPTEMBER 09, 2017

One person died and a dozen were injured in violent clashes between local residents and policemen outside the Ramganj police station in the Walled City of Jaipur late on Friday. Curfew has been clamped in the areas falling within the jurisdiction of four police stations in the city, and mobile internet services suspended for 48 hours.

The violence erupted when a policeman allegedly hit a man riding a motorcycle with a baton during a routine vehicle check and misbehaved with the motorist's wife. Following an altercation with the police personnel, hundreds of people, who had gathered at the spot, rushed to the police station and pelted stones.

The police resorted to a lathi charge and lobbed teargas shells to disperse the crowd, which went on the rampage and torched about twenty vehicles, including an ambulance and a police van. Several policemen were also injured in the violence. As the situation went out of control, the police personnel reportedly fired in the air to disperse the crowd. A twenty-two-year-old man, identified as Mohammed Rais alias Adil, was injured in the firing. The police said he died late at night. Among the injured policemen, one was stated to be in critical condition and was admitted to the Intensive Care Unit of the Sawai Man Singh Government Hospital.

https://www.thehindu.com/news/national/violence-rocks-jaipur-1-dies/article19651893.ece

UP: Mob goes on rampage after car runs over 4-year-old boy

TNN | OCT 12, 2019

ALLAHABAD: A four-year-old boy was run over by a speeding car near Nehru Park Road late on Thursday night, triggering large-scale protests during which a mob vandalized two vehicles, including the official car of the additional city magistrate, and pelted stones that left three policemen injured.

The area under Cantonment police station continued to remain tense on Friday, prompting heavy police deployment. Four inebriated youths who were in the killer car have been arrested.

Sources in the police said the deceased child had been identified as Yuvraj, a resident of Cantonment area. He had stepped out of his home to relieve himself when he was run over by the drunk youths. Yuvraj was cremated at a local ghat amid tight security on Friday.

Police said the angry mob not only ransacked the magistrate's car, but also attacked the driver of a crane and a constable who had gone to tow away the car that caused the fatal accident.

https://timesofindia.indiatimes.com/city/allahabad/mob-goes-on-rampage-after-car-runs-over-4-year-old-boy/articleshowprint/71546984.cms

PROLOGUE
Inside

Lub-dub-lub-dub …

The booming from inside her chest was furious and incessant. It rose above the tumult around her: roars; wails; bangs; clangs; crackles; thuds; groans.

Dub-lub-dub-lub …

She licked her cracked lips, caked with dust and ash, and spat out brown spittle. Her breath came in rapid wheezes as she wrinkled her nose against the acrid smoke and fine ash floating in the dark air. She squeezed her eyes shut and frantically wiped away the tears with the back of her pudgy hand.

'Nafisa?'

'*What*, Murad?' Nafisa frowned at the little boy holding her other hand. With his big, round eyes bedewed with tears, his scrawny neck bent all the way backward over his bony shoulders to look up at her, he looked tinier and more frail than usual. Gently, she dabbed away the fresh blood that had oozed out of the small cut on his left cheek, then wiped her finger clean on her frock, which was already stained with blood.

'Ammi?' Murad whimpered.

'Shh, shh,' Nafisa hissed and squeezed his hand hard. 'Don't make a noise.'

'Pee,' Murad whispered.

Nafisa sighed, looked around the room and cautiously led him to the toilet at the back of the dingy storeroom lined with shelves laden with fabric and readymade garments. She helped him out of his grubby shorts and ushered him into the toilet.

'You will soon be two—you should learn how to take off and wear your own clothes, stupid,' she said, as she waited for him outside.

'Done!' Murad announced.

'Wash your hands and come out fast.'

'Why do I need to wash my hands?'

'Because I am your elder sister and I said so,' Nafisa snapped. 'Doesn't Ammi always say that you should listen to your big sister?'

Their bickering was interrupted by sudden crashing sounds outside the bolted doorway, near the toilet, followed by an explosive whoosh. Nafisa rushed into the toilet to find the boy staring at a small ventilator window near the ceiling. They could see the bright, high flames outside throwing up balls of oily smoke.

Nafisa dragged the half-dressed Murad out of the toilet and slammed the door shut. She yanked up his shorts, hurried him to a corner of the storeroom and made him sit on a carton of t-shirts.

Pointing a strict forefinger at her brother, Nafisa stepped hesitantly towards the narrow passage that led to the back door. Flashes of red and orange strobed from the gap under the door; wisps of smoke seeped in through the cracks, making her cough. Dashing back to the storeroom, she rummaged through the racks of clothes. She found a pile of flimsy cotton towels, pulled out two and rushed to the toilet. Turning on the tap in the washbasin, she drenched the towels.

'Nafisa?' Murad whined from the corner.

'Stay there if you don't want to be slapped!' Nafisa yelled over her shoulder.

She ran back to the door and plugged a wet towel into the finger-thick gap under it. Coughing furiously, she hung the second towel over some nails jutting out of the rough wood. It covered a crack—about six-inches long—at the side of the door.

Stepping back, she eyed her handiwork with pursed lips and narrowed, watery eyes. The smoke entering the room had reduced considerably. She had just turned and started to walk towards Murad when she stopped dead in her tracks. A loud bang—like a big firecracker—came from outside the shopfront.

Nafisa had heard the noise before—on the night when Ammi and Khalid Mamu had taken her and Murad out to the sprawling graveyard nearby. Khalid Mamu had brought a big, round flatbread in a cardboard box. Nafisa had loved it. It was cut into triangles and had many different food items stuck on top. It was crunchy, juicy and had a strange mix of tastes—from tangy to sweet and hot. The bread had chicken pieces too, in the form of small discs. She had never eaten anything like that before.

Ammi and Khalid Mamu were drinking some smelly, brownish liquid from a bottle he had brought. Ammi had looked so happy that night. She always looked happy when Khalid Mamu gave her that drink. But sometimes it also made her very sad and cry.

After some time, Ammi asked Khalid Mamu for something, and he took out a small metal pipe with a handle at one end. He had laughed and pointed the thing at a gnarled tree. Then, BANG! The flash and the loud noise made Nafisa's ears ring so bad that she covered her ears. She could see Murad cry. There was a jagged hole in the tree trunk, Nafisa noticed. Khalid Mamu scooped her up and hoisted her on his shoulders while Ammi carried Murad and they had all fled the graveyard. Ammi kept laughing all the way home.

The bang she heard from within the storeroom had sounded just like that night. Nafisa remembered the jagged hole in the tree. She rushed to her brother and hugged him tightly. There was a moment of absolute silence outside, then she heard enraged cries, angry shouts … and another bang. She felt Murad's shoulders convulse and she gripped him tighter.

'Ammi …' her brother choked.

'Shh, shh!'

Nafisa struggled to keep their voices down. She heard screams, sound of shuffling feet, loud thuds and thumps. There were grunts, moans and curses. There was the sound of metal scraping the pavement. The deafening crash of glass shattering. The rattling of the metal grill at the entrance to the shop. The roar of a frenzied mob approaching, faint at first but increasing in pitch and intensity till it engulfed them like a hurricane.

Nafisa pulled her brother's head to her chest, wrapping her arms around him as though to shield him from the pandemonium outside. She squeezed her eyes shut against the blinding flashes that assaulted them. She could feel his skin pucker up with goosebumps as she waited …

PART ONE
Stoned

1

A fresh gust of wind disturbs the stillness under the brutal summer sun. A lone leaf shudders and detaches from a drooping twig and floats down the leathery grey trunk of the jamun tree. It flips over on the sandstone pavement with a dry click, which ripples in the searing air, and then comes to rest, wedged under a small stone.

Ali does not look older than nine or ten. He leans against the tree trunk in a tiny patch of shade, smoking. He peers at the leaf, his yellowed eyes squinting through the mop of unruly curls bleached from the sun. The scarlet-and-blue FC Barcelona jersey he wears has '10' and 'MESSI' stencilled on the back and pinhole burns all over the front. It sticks to his spindly frame, glistening with sweat.

He adjusts the bundle of cellophane-wrapped books and a few packets of sketch pens and ballpoints in the crook of his left arm, then takes a last pull of the cigarette and flicks it away. Slipping off his right sneaker without laces, Ali slides his foot across the flagstone and pinches the fallen leaf between his toes. He retrieves the leaf from under the stone, taking care to remain in the relative shade of the tree. Placing his bundle on the ground, he picks up the leaf. There is a strange pattern on it that looks like 'Khalid' in Urdu. Ali smiles at how well he can read now.

Frowning in concentration, he inserts the leaf into his torn shoes to cover a small hole in the sole. With his feet protected from the burning concrete of the pavement, he takes a tentative step out of the shade. His chapped lips are stretched in a pleased grin, as he begins pacing the pavement to sell his wares.

2

The beer café, across the road and overlooking the intersection, is overcrowded, noisy and stuffy. Angad Gill pokes a finger inside his starched-white shirt collar and scratches his neck, gritty from dust. He looks up at the air-conditioner. The display shows 26°C. With a sigh, he loosens the knot of his scarlet tie and takes a sip of chilled beer. He looks through the French window beside him at the street outside shimmering under the blazing sun.

Dust devils whip up dry leaves and bits of litter that rattle against the glass and fall on the ground, defeated. The urchin selling pirated books at the crossing struts up and down the pavement, impervious to the heat. Their eyes meet, and the boy grins at Angad who waves back.

Thoi sips her lemon iced tea and looks at Angad, her dark eyes spilling love. She takes in his straight nose, unibrow under a high forehead and grey eyes. The prescription summer mufti and his crisp, maroon turban make him look dashing. Thoi pushes her shoulder-length hair off her smooth, heart-shaped face with its delicate bone structure. Leaning forward, she touches Angad's arm lightly, making him turn to her.

'Qu'est-ce que c'est? What's so fascinating outside?' she asks.

'That boy,' says Angad, nodding at the boy from the window. Thoi's dreamy, wide-set eyes follow his. Across the road, she spots Ali beneath the tree, picking up his bundle of books and pens.

'He might be among the wretched of this earth but at least he's trying to make a living,' Angad adds. 'I say, a soldier fighting against poverty.'

Thoi smiles, her even white teeth peeping out from behind her full lips.

'My soldier philosopher! Je t'aime.'

'Only a Gentleman Cadet from National Defence Academy with some thoughts,' Angad quips, taking another sip of his beer. 'And please don't intimidate me with your French just because you're doing your masters in the subject. It scares me.'

Thoi laughs.

'I say—do you have beggars in the Northeast, Thoi?'

'You mean my state, right?' Thoi says, her smile changing to a scowl. She draws her hand back and straightens her slim frame. 'I can only speak for my home state. You all just club the whole region as if it were one big blob on the map.'

Angad puts his beer down and looks at her. He takes in her delicate features, pale smoothness and slim frame accentuated by her fitted, short summer dress. He tilts his head and nods slowly, putting up his palms in a reconciliatory gesture. 'You're so beautiful,' he says with a disarming smile.

Thoi's pursed lips melt into a lopsided smile. 'Merci. And we don't have beggars in my state.'

'Umm … yeah—we are not all "chinkies"—umm … as you guys call everyone from the Northeast,' Bonium speaks up from behind them, through a mouthful of tandoori prawns. He is what Angad calls an 'all-rounder': round face, round eyes, round belly.

'What the hell do you mean by "you guys"?' Angad asks with a frown. 'And I thought you were on a diet!'

'Let my little cousin be, Angad,' Thoi admonishes. 'The poor guy has been surviving on fruits and salads for a week. I told him he can eat whatever he wants today—in honour of you graduating from the academy.'

Angad laughs and thumps Bonium on the back. He drains his glass of beer and orders another pitcher for everyone.

'So, when do you join the army?' asks Karl. His khadi bush shirt, jeans, ponytail and beard scream 'intellectual', or so he thinks.

'Dude—I'm *already* in the Indian Army,' Angad responds. 'You're a reporter now, you should have your facts right. I will join the Military Academy next week and get *commissioned* in a year.'

'We feel so proud of you, bro. An army officer and all that!' says Raunak, enthusiastically. 'And to think that we were all in school together just a few years back.'

'And now Partho is making ads for laxatives,' Uma sniggers, poking Partho in the ribs with her fat, GRE practice book. 'The quintessential artsy-fartsy Bengali,' she says, speaking with a slow drawl, her 't's and 'd's tumbled out more emphatically.

'At least I'm doing something productive for the country,' Partho retorts. 'Not like you South Indians, who just want to somehow get to the US.'

'Hey! I am from "South India" too,' Karl protests. 'But I dislike the US and all their worshipping of corporate Molochs.'

'Well, we're better than Raunak at least—just living off his ancestral land,' Uma makes a face at Partho. 'Or Karl here, who's hoping for a Bolshevik Revolution and ranting against everything and everyone creating wealth. He's like a typical Keralite, the last samurai of communism!' She says so while rolling her wide, fish-shaped eyes lined with kohl.

'Talking of wealth,' Angad says hastily, trying to avoid the inevitable debate that would follow on capitalism, patriotism, regionalism and so many other isms his friends love to argue over. 'Check out that Orca Black Audi Q7 approaching the signal.'

3

Malaika flicks the stub of her cigarette out of the window of her Orca Black Audi Q7, and quickly rolls up the tinted glass against the swirling dust and heat. She adjusts her blue Prada shades and unbuttons the Chinese collar of her dress, before crossing her shapely long legs sheathed in grey slacks. She could easily pass off as a decade younger than her thirty-four years. Her thin, arched eyebrows and Greek nose give her a distinctly patrician look.

'Suraj, turn up the fan speed, please,' she commands. In the front seat, Suraj reaches out to twist the knob clockwise till the reading shows '7' on the panel, his eyes firmly on the road. Even though this is not his car, he loves driving it and does not mind Malaika's tone.

'Looks like there's a traffic jam ahead,' he observes, slowing down as he approaches the signal. He adjusts his squat, muscular frame and edges closer to the steering wheel, shoulders hunched in impatience. His toned biceps twitch under the short sleeves of his black t-shirt. His rectangular face, with narrow, wide-set eyes under thick eyebrows, the snub and slightly crooked nose and broad straight lips, sits above a square jaw, giving him a pugnacious look. The elongated vermilion tilak on his forehead makes him look like a mediaeval warrior.

'Priscilla, are you sure the fellow has 160 by 90, C50 by C50 cotton twill?' Malaika asks the lean and trim woman in her late twenties sitting in the passenger seat in front of her. 'Lorna is very particular, aren't you?' she adds, turning to the woman sitting next to her.

'Mais oui!' both Priscilla and Lorna answer together and burst out laughing.

'Stop fretting so much, Malaika,' Lorna pats Malaika's arm. She looks older than Malaika, but her face has a pleasant fullness about it. When she smiles, a little dimple pools below her left cheekbone. She is impeccably dressed in a white top and fuchsia pencil skirt that hug her lithe and curvaceous figure and a muslin scarf draped around her long neck. 'Your buying house has worked for us for over three years and has always got us what we want. You do a great job for us in Southeast Asia.'

'Well, last time you guys made such a fuss over the NE-count of the fabric I had procured. That bitch, Colette, gave me hell. She thinks she knows fabrics just because she's French,' Malaika snarls, her lips quivering.

'Well, well, well … we all know how exasperating Colette can get,' Lorna says in a soothing voice. 'That's what QC folks do. But this time she has already approved the sample. So … just relax. She used to be nasty to me—even though I'm French like her, uh, at least French-American. I thought it was because I'm black. But later I realized that she was … just a born bitch.'

Everyone laughs.

'Look, Malaika,' Priscilla says, twisting in her seat to face her boss and holding up a fabric sample. 'As your procurement manager, I have done fibre, fabric, yarn testing and—'

'I know,' Malaika cuts her off. 'I just don't want to take any more shit from that snooty bitch this time for no fault of ours. I'm livid. And what's the matter with you, Suraj? As the sales head, you should be even more desperate to get Lorna to sign the deal—no? Just honk your damn way through this traffic. We're running late. Those silly suppliers will shut for their prayers by noon and then for lunch. And that's despite me telling them we have Lorna coming all the way from Brussels for approval. So bloody unprofessional!'

'Oh, *those* folks are incorrigible,' Suraj says over his shoulder, while aggressively pressing the horn. He touches the vermilion tilak on his forehead. 'I hate doing business with *them*. Bloody religious fundamentalists.'

'Oh, come on,' Priscilla protests. 'They have a right to practise their religion. We *are* a secular country, no? Or do you also resent for me being a Christian who attends Sunday mass at church? Why are *you* wearing that big red tilak? Don't be such a bigot.'

'I went to the temple this morning to pray for my newborn niece,' Suraj mutters under his breath.

But Lorna's attention is diverted by something outside the window. 'Zinga ice cream!' she exclaims. 'I just love 'em. Haven't had it since my last visit … in February? Suraj—will you please stop when we reach that cart?'

4

Hari Shankar wipes his creased, sun-baked brows with a rag. Across the road, he sees Ali tap his bundle of books and raise four fingers. Hari Shankar smiles and nods.

The traffic has started to pile up. Ahead of the signal, Khalid and his men are spreading out durries for the Dhuhr namaz. Hari Shankar kicks away the stones from under the wheels of his ice cream cart, edges it closer to the road and parks on the pavement, next to the auto stand. Traffic jams are always good for business. He nods and smiles at the two auto drivers, regulars in the area, waiting for passengers at the stand.

Ali is pacing along the pavement, knocking on car windows, pressing books against the windows of halted cars. Sometimes, his open smile earns one in return, sometimes an angry frown, but mostly the eyes inside do not turn to look at him. His shrill voice doesn't pierce the glass wall that divides those who scream and those who cannot hear.

'Ali! Ali!' Hari Shankar calls out. 'You have done good business. Four books are very good. Come and have an ice cream. For free!' He takes out a popsicle and waves it at the boy.

Ali gestures he can't hear Hari Shankar over the din of traffic but nods back, licking his lips in anticipation of the treat. He rushes forward as a car window comes down. He fans out his books and holds them up against the glass.

'Where is Khan Khana restaurant?' asks a man gruffly.

5

Bashir Khan stands under the awning outside his restaurant, Khan Khana. The bright signboard declares proudly: 'Established in 1919 by Khan Babrak Khan of Nuristan'. He looks up at the sign and kisses his fingertips in reverence. 'Thank you, Ghor-neeka Khan,' he murmurs, remembering his great-grandfather with reverence. 'I hope you are content with how I have handled your legacy these past two decades since you asked me to move from Afghanistan after dear plaar passed away.'

He doffs the pakol cap, uncovering his shaved pate beaded with perspiration. His flowing salt-and-pepper beard cascades down to his chest and the drooping moustache almost hides his thin lips. His face is narrow and pinched and his brooding eyes bulge above prominent bags. The white muslin pathan suit he is wearing is crisply ironed but the creases have gone a little limp with sweat.

He looks across the street to where his boys are spreading out durries for the noon prayer on the pavement in front of Khalid's motorcycle repair shop. Khalid looks up and raises a hand to his forehead. Bashir nods and half-raises his hand in return.

He looks to his left and finds Vinod Mehra standing outside his garment shop with Sonu, one of his shop assistants. A handful of workers are setting up monster speakers at the entrance to Mehra's shop. The workers have just put up a banner announcing the night-long programme of bhajans and puja. Bashir turns his head away as Mehra looks sidelong at him with a wicked grin. Someone inside Mehra's shop turns on the speakers.

'Hello, hello, hello! Mic testing, mic testing, one, two, three, testing …'

The speakers screech and echo, making Bashir grit his teeth. From across the street, he sees Khalid and his boys looking askance at him. Bashir checks his watch. It is almost noon. The call for prayers will begin in a few minutes.

The speakers from Mehra's shop blare to life with a bhajan. Bashir glares at Mehra but the shopkeeper deliberately turns his back to him. He takes a step towards Mehra, then halts, scratching his shaggy beard. He looks at the PCR van parked at the curb diagonally across the street, near the traffic signal. Sub-Inspector Satpal leans against the bonnet of the vehicle, reading a newspaper. Gulshan, the aged head constable is in the driver's seat, dozing. A few feet away, Constable Kultar Singh is talking on his cell phone, absently swinging his cane. The traffic constable, Amit is slouching against a wall staring at the pile-up of vehicles with a bored expression. Bashir shakes his head in disgust.

A boisterous group of African students emerge from an alley and swarm past Bashir, laughing, hooting and hopping around. A strapping young man is shadow-boxing, making the two girls in the group giggle. The youth bumps into Bashir, causing him to drop his pakol on the dusty pavement.

'Sorry, old man!' the boy says over his shoulder, without breaking his stride.

Bashir roars out an expletive. The three African boys turn around making offensive gestures with their fingers and strut away, the girls giggling even harder.

6

Sub-Inspector Satpal Choudhary looks up from his newspaper at the source of the commotion. He is a lanky, tall man with deep-set eyes, thin lips that taper down at the corners and jet-black hair with hints of grey at the temples. His every movement portrays jaded lethargy and utter disinterest.

Satpal watches Bashir shake his fist and scream at a group of students. He blinks against the flying dust stinging his eyes and folds away his newspaper. Putting on his imitation Ray-Ban shades, Satpal watches Khalid run across the street to talk to Bashir. The two confer animatedly, with Bashir jabbing his finger several times towards the students, already entering the pub down the street. Khalid takes a step forward in the direction of the students, but Bashir puts a restraining hand on his shoulder. He points at his watch and pats Khalid on the shoulder.

Satpal observes as Khalid returns to the group of mechanics and vendors who pray together. He calls out to Kultar, who disconnects his call and walks over.

'Stay alert,' Satpal warns. 'Mehra is starting his show now—he has permission from the station head. And Bashir looks upset. I am tired of the daily fights between Mehra and Bashir.'

'Sir, Mehra does these all-night public pujas every few months,' Kultar says, shrugging. 'What's so—'

'—Mehra has always started the puja after six in the evening—just an overnight affair. Today ... Mehra's speakers will drown the afternoon azan. I think it is to rile Bashir whose cousin lost the municipal election to Mehra's uncle. They think they are world leaders or something. Like Kim and Putin—bloody megalomaniacs. And it is fucking hot today! Even my butt crack is dripping with sweat. I don't want any stupid fight here. Keep an eye on them.'

'Okay, sir,' Kultar shrugs again.

'And watch that Khalid—the prick thinks he's some film star. Also, that fatso sidekick of Mehra—Bindal. They are all trouble. The bastards. I want to beat the shit out of these motherfuckers one day.'

'Who was Bashir shouting at?' Kultar asks.

'How will you know if you are fucking glued to your phone all the time?' Satpal asks testily. 'A bunch of African students said or did something to anger him. I'm sick of those black pigs too. Drugs, whoring ... always shitting around everywhere. Why the fuck does the government even allow those blackies into our country? Fucking globalization! I'm just going into that pub to check out their papers—maybe Bashir will see me do that and feel a little pacified. His nephew is an MLA. Through Bashir, I may be able to get his nephew's help for a posting in the transport department, which I have been trying to get for so long. This post is a fucking pain in the arse, I swear.'

Kultar nods as Satpal walks away, tapping the Glock 17 in its tan leather holster on his hip.

'And ask that traffic runt to do something about the mess at the signal,' he hollers out.

7

'We haven't moved an inch in the past five minutes,' Malaika groans, dabbing her face with a wet tissue.

'It's those buggers,' Suraj points at Khalid and his group getting ready to offer namaz. 'They've blocked half the bloody street. They think they own the bloody country. Look at that old baboon shaking his fists and screaming at those black monkeys!'

'Suraj! Watch your fucking mouth,' Malaika whacks him on the head.

'Uh—sorry. I meant …' he stammers, fidgeting with his gold chain and the Om pendant on it.

'That's all right, guys,' Lorna says with a thin smile. 'I've heard African students have a bad reputation here. I guess, people here don't quite like—'

'It's not just them, Lorna,' Priscilla interjects. 'It's us Northeasterners as well. That fellow screaming at the students probably thinks of us as the dregs too. To them, all the men are pimps and all the girls are sluts. Last month, I was at a party at a friend's place. I stepped out to the terrace for a smoke and this guy followed me out and asked me what I charge for a night. Just because I—I look different? Can you believe that? Assholes … just like this Suraj here.'

'Hey! C'mon now, Pris,' Suraj said with an exaggerated groan. 'Who slapped that drunk fucker for you?'

'You did,' Priscilla says, throwing her head back against the headrest. 'You're still an asshole.'

'This mama wants ice cream, Sooooraaaj,' Lorna croons, with a laugh.

'And she will get it,' Malaika says, laughing awkwardly. 'But reserve some space for a lunch treat from Suraj after our meeting.'

'Oh! Really' Lorna smiles. 'What's the treat for?'

'I have become an uncle today,' Suraj grins into the rear view. 'My older sister-in-law had a baby girl this morning. They live in Australia.'

'Wow! Congratulations,' Lorna says, patting Suraj on his shoulder. 'Is that why you have that … that red paint on your forehead?'

'It's a tika,' Malaika explains. 'He was late picking us up because he went to a temple to offer prayers for his newborn niece.'

'I love girls,' Suraj says, nodding his head.

'Don't we all know that?' Priscilla snorts.

'Heck! Not like that,' Suraj protests. 'For two generations, my dad's family only had boys. I always wanted a sister when I was growing up. And I want a daughter one day. They make life beautiful.'

'Aww, that's so sweet,' Lorna croons. 'Who would've guessed? So why don't you make your own baby girl?'

'I have to find the right oven for that first,' Suraj screws up his face and guffaws, flicking away a strand of straight, wispy hair from his forehead.

'Bloody chauvinist pig,' Priscilla says, slapping Suraj on his arm. 'Disgusting! And we know you've already found it. We're just waiting for the announcement.'

8

Titus slips off his Armani shades and flops on the settee in the hookah section of the pub. He rolls up the long sleeves of his t-shirt, revealing his taut forearms, and pats the space next to him, smiling at Faith. She slides into the booth and leans against Titus. He runs a finger lightly on her bare thighs and feels the holes and tears of her distressed-denim shorts. Faith pushes his hand away with a righteous frown.

Her younger friend, Sharon stands undecided near the table till Victor gallantly pulls out a chair for her. She smiles at him and sits down. Grinning, Victor feints a punch at his classmate Idris, who pretends to swoon and slumps into another chair. Victor waves at the waiter who hurries across from the counter.

'And which beers do you have on the tap, yo?' Victor asks, clapping a gnarled hand with blackened knuckles on the waiter's shoulder.

'Sir, we have light beers like—'

'None of that, yo!' Victor cuts the waiter off. 'We're, like, *ce-le-bra-ting*, man. See this guy?' He points at Titus. 'He's got a scholarship to Cornell! He's a dude, yo? D'you have a stronger beer?'

The waiter nods.

'Then bring that—for all of us.'

'Hey, I'm not drinkin', man!' Idris protests. 'I have my student counselling at 3 p.m. at the university.'

'Yes, you *are*.' Victor shakes a stern finger at Idris. 'Didn't you hear? We're ce-le-bra-ting, yo?'

Idris relents and puts up his hands as a show of surrender. Victor grins and sits down.

'We're all so proud of you, Titus,' Faith says, putting her arms around Titus. 'Sends a big message to the university crowd. We're not trash, no we ain't!'

Titus nods slowly and smiles. Victor and Idris lean forward to bump fists with Titus.

'Yeah, it's a huge opportunity,' Titus sighs. 'Sadly, we don't have … uh … such colleges and universities in Kenya. I'm glad I listened to my dad—for once—and came to India for higher studies. Even the coaching centres for GRE or GMAT are so much better here … and … umm … affordable. Hope some of you can make it to a good course in the US next year.'

'Amen to that!' Faith chimes.

The waiter places pints of beer on the table and pops open the bottles.

'Cheers! To Titus and Ivy League colleges!' Victor roars, raising his bottle.

'And to India!' Titus adds. They clink their bottles and raise them above their heads before taking quick sips.

Angad and his friends sitting at the next table turn to them with smiles and raise their own glasses.

9

Sub-Inspector Satpal walks down the pavement past the intersection. The flower girl, Fatima is sitting right under the pedestrian signal yet again. He frowns and stops.

'Haven't I told you many times not to sit here?' Satpal growls at the young woman.

'Sahib, this is the best place to sell my flowers. I can't leave my children and run after people,' Fatima replies, putting a hand on her two-year-old son's head. Her five-year-old daughter is playing with a plastic doll a few feet away. Fatima has a delicate, oval face. Though light-skinned, she looks like burnt toast from spending years under the sun. Her hair is matted and skin full of scratches and scabs.

Satpal glares at Fatima for a long moment. The flowers and marigold garlands in her plastic basket look sad and withered. The toddler looks unclean and hungry, chewing on an empty plastic water bottle. The little girl looks grimy, with strings of dry hair hanging around her hollow face. Catching Satpal's gaze, the child smiles. He gives an exasperated sigh.

'Why don't you go to some other intersection, near a temple, where people actually buy flowers?' he asks.

'Sahib, because of my brother—Ali,' Fatima answers, pointing at the boy peddling books and pens near the crossing. 'Here he can sell eight to ten books in a day for that ice cream man. Sometimes even a dozen. He gets a commission of Rs 10 on every book. That's a lot of money. No one buys books at a temple.'

Satpal knows them all. He has seen Ali run up and down the street day after day, laughing, making people laugh and selling his pirated books and cheap Chinese pens. He glares at Fatima and her two kids. She looks like a kid herself, he thinks.

'You ought to be in some school, studying,' he growls. 'Not sitting here blocking the pavement with your litter.'

Fatima laughs sardonically and offers a wilted stick of rajnigandha to the policeman. Satpal looks in silence at her challenging, mirthless eyes and crooked teeth behind chapped lips. The purple bruise on her cheekbone could only have been from a hard slap or a punch. He takes a deep breath and walks away with purposeful strides. A few steps ahead, he climbs up the shallow stairs to the door of the pub. The doorman salutes and pushes open the heavy wooden door for the policeman.

10

Pramod Bindal smiles as he hears the bhajans blaring from the loudspeakers next door. He reaches into the drawer below his cash counter and shoves away an assortment of knives, ice-picks and knuckle dusters. Finally, he takes out a hidden steel tiffin box. He opens the lid and selects a besan laddoo to eat. He closes his eyes as the crunchy sweetness floods his palate.

'Vikas, Punit?'

His shop assistants look up from the racks of hardware they are inventorying.

'I am just stepping across to Mehra's shop,' Bindal informs through a mouthful of laddoo. 'The keys of the cash box are in the drawer. Understand?'

The two young men look at each other and grin. 'We understand,' they chorus.

'Good. It should be a fun day today,' Bindal continues, wiping his mouth with a pink handkerchief. 'The puja will begin in a while. Free food for all. The cooks are good—I know them. And that asshole Bashir will be furious because of the puja.'

'Yes, yes,' Vikas and Punit chirp, nodding vigorously as they continue working.

'Every day, Khalid and those buggers block the road as if their fathers own it. I don't know why they don't go back to where they belong. Today, we will show them who the boss is. Understand?'

'Yes, yes.'

'The senior inspector has given Mehra permission to play bhajans on loudspeakers till midnight, understand?' Mehra grunts, squeezing his heavy frame through the narrow gap behind the cash counter. 'Why not? I supplied all the paint and POP for his new apartment. The inspector owes me some favours. I just want to watch Bashir and Khalid suffer a little, understand?'

'Yes, yes.'

Bindal steps out of his shop on to the pavement and looks around. Khalid and his men have occupied half the street with their durries, causing traffic at the intersection. The lone traffic constable is trying to clear the congestion, blowing his whistle furiously and gesticulating with both his hands at drivers.

Bindal sees Satpal walk up to the pub with a dark expression. He waves but the policeman does not notice him. Bindal looks to his left where that old man Hari Sankar is standing next to his ice cream cart, chatting with a couple of auto drivers. Bindal checks his watch. The free puja lunch is still an hour away. He licks his lips and starts walking towards Hari Shankar's cart.

11

Satpal squeezes his eyes to adjust his vision to the relative darkness inside the pub. He inhales deeply, savouring the cool air. The manager scurries across the room to meet him.

'Sir, is everything all right?'

Satpal nods, looks around and spots the group of African youngsters. He pushes past the manager and marches to their table.

'Hello,' he says gruffly, standing behind Victor. 'Can I see some identifications?'

There is a long silence as everyone at the table looks at the police officer. Satpal stares back and extends an open palm.

'Why?' Titus finally asks.

Satpal arches his back and looks hard at the young man. He tilts his head to the left and then to the right.

'Because I am asking,' he speaks each word one by one, with his hands on his hips and legs planted apart. 'Don't try to be smart with me. I need to verify if you have valid documents.'

Titus takes out his wallet and hands his university ID to Satpal. The others wait without moving.

'MA student, political science,' Satpal reads out. 'It doesn't have a visa stamp, asshole.' Saying so, he throws the ID on the table.

Victor tries to get up but Titus gestures, him to back down. Quietly, he retrieves his ID and places it next to his bottle of beer—in plain sight. Satpal waits for some response, but Titus goes back to sipping his beer.

'What are you doing with these women?' Satpal snaps. 'What do they do?'

'They,' Titus answers, looking the policeman in the eye, 'are all students at the university. She,' he continues, pointing at Faith, 'is doing a post-graduation in microbiology. My other friends are in undergraduate courses. We are all foreign students.'

'*Foreign?*' Satpal sniggers. 'Like from England, America, Canada, Australia?'

'I'm from Kenya,' Titus replies. 'It is a country in Africa, you know? Kenya has an embassy in India. She is from Botswana, those two are from Namibia and that friend is from Gabon—all countries in Africa. Yes, we are all *foreign* students.'

'Embassy, huh?' Satpal snorts. 'Trying to intimidate me, are you?'

Titus says nothing but pulls out his cell phone and puts it down on the table. He does not break eye contact with the policeman. Another long moment of silence passes, with both men staring at each other without a blink.

'What are you doing here?' Satpal breaks the silence.

'Yo man, we're celebrating,' Victor interjects.

'Why? Is it your father's wedding today?'

'Titus has got a full scholarship to an American university,' Faith butts in hastily, before Victor can react. 'Please, sir, we are just students.'

'Excuse me,' a voice carries from the table near a big glass window. Satpal squints and spots a group of Indians. He sighs heavily and turns to them.

'What?'

A slim young Sikh walks towards Satpal, ducking his head to avoid a low wooden beam of the ceiling. His Oxfords are shiny and click loudly on the polished floor.

'Sub-Inspector,' Angad says, standing across from Satpal and scrutinizing the policeman's shoulder insignias. They both stand towering over the table, eye to eye. He extends a hand. 'GC Angad Gill.'

'GC?'

'Gentleman Cadet,' Angad says pleasantly. 'I've just graduated from the National Defence Academy. Joining the Indian Military Academy next week.'

Satpal looks at the natty boy and scratches his two-day-old stubble. He ignores the extended hand.

'Yes?'

'I—we are also celebrating,' Angad says smiling. 'My graduation.'

'And …?'

'And this man has been accepted to—uh—attend a famous university in the US. I just heard him thank our country for making it possible. And they are our guests. We should treat them nicely, no? This is what India stands for—I say.'

Satpal looks at Angad's appearance. Then he looks at the pretty girls sitting at the other table, drinking alcohol, wearing short dresses. He stares at Thoi for a moment.

'You say? Do you understand what India stands for? What do *you* do for the country, huh?' Satpal asks dryly.

'I ... we defend the country,' Angad says, looking perplexed.

'From drug dealers?' Satpal snarls. 'Pimps, prostitutes, thieves?'

Angad says nothing.

'Do you catch murderers? Rapists? Burglars? Arsonists?' Satpal presses on.

'We protect India from enemies, so you can sleep in peace,' Angad says, his face flushed and fists clenched.

'It's not 12 as yet,' Satpal smirks, looking at his watch and shaking his head. 'What do Sardars do at 12? Sleep? "Protect country"… hah! Murderers and rapists are your friends? Burglars sing lullabies for you? Tell me, are your mother and sister threatened every day by the enemy across the border or the enemy within? Please tell me, Sardar ji?'

'Listen, Sub-Inspector—' Angad's face is flushed, his eyes narrowed into slits.

'No! *You* listen, army boy,' Satpal hisses, thrusting his chin forward. '*I* don't come interfering when you are playing golf at your club, drinking subsidized whisky at your mess or shooting across the border from behind sandbags. So, don't *you* interfere when I am trying to do *my* job.'

'How dare you speak of the Army in—'

'—how *dare* I?' Satpal shouts. 'Look at that wretched woman outside—walking towards the ice cream stall with that plastic bucket of rotting flowers. And look at that boy trying to sell books at the signal. They are siblings. She lives on the street with her two children. In the last four months, there have been three rape attempts on her. *My* men stopped it. *I* have put those bastards behind bars. It is because of *me* and *my* men that she can sleep peacefully, even if it is on hard stones. And you say *you* understand India? That *you* defend her? And what do *I* do? Get my arse fucked all day?'

Satpal whips around and faces Titus.

'I hate pimps, prostitutes and druggies,' he spits out. 'All of you are the same. Finish your celebration quickly and get out of my area. I know what you fellows do—and what these women do at night. I tolerate no trash in my jurisdiction. Get out fast before I take you all in for questioning.'

Before anyone can react, he turns on his heels and walks out of the pub.

12

Ramji rests an elbow on the rod in his auto that separates the passenger section from the driver's. His t-shirt's collar is turned up and a colourful linen kerchief is stuck under the collar to soak up sweat. He takes puffs from his beedi as he reads the newspaper spread across his folded knees.

'Listen to this,' he says, glancing at the auto driver parked right behind him. They were idling at the spot near the traffic light, just under the 'AUTO STAND' signage. 'This year, the chief minister will attend the Chhath puja ceremonies and offer prayers to the sun!' He has to speak loudly to be heard over the devotional songs from Mehra's loudspeakers and the incessant honking and the rumbling of engines from the street.

The other auto driver, Deepak leans against his own auto and enjoys a stick of ice cream. He grunts and keeps licking his stick, nodding to the rhythm of the bhajans wafting through the air.

'It was expected,' Hari Shankar chuckles, wiping the shiny aluminium top of his cart near the auto parking spot. 'Elections are coming up next year. Migrants like us have to be wooed.' He shakes his head.

'These two-faced bloody politicians!' Deepak speaks in between loud slurps. 'At functions and before the media they curse us—blame us migrants for overcrowding the city and increasing the crime rate. Incidents of rape have gone up because of *us*, they say. We are a burden on the city, they imply. When they want votes from the locals, they promise to throw us back to where we came from. These bastards. And when it is time for elections, they attend our pujas and functions and tell us *our* labour is helping the city develop and that *we* contribute to the city's economy. The fork-tongued snakes.' He finishes his ice cream and throws the stick on the pavement.

'Maybe we are not wanted here,' Hari Shankar says as he quietly picks up the stick and puts it in a cardboard carton he keeps for trash.

The traffic mess has worsened. A shiny black SUV is stuck a few cars away, in the opposite lane. The two autos parked at the curb on Hari Shankar's side are adding to the mess. The SUV emits a few impatient honks and they see the driver making an angry gesture at them for blocking a lane, demanding they move away.

'Really?' Deepak snarls, ignoring the SUV. 'And how will the middle-class commute, if we auto rickshaw drivers go back? In fancy cars like that one? Look at that bastard in that fancy SUV glaring at us from inside his AC car. As if his father owns the road. I want to smash the damn window and then smash that man's teeth. He's just showing off to those women sitting in that car. Lucky bastard, he has a blackie and a chinkie with him. Oooh, I wish I could—'

'—that sub-inspector just came out of that pub,' Ramji says, folding up his paper and nodding towards the pub. 'He seems to be in a foul mood. Better not smash any teeth right now.'

13

'Hey, thanks man,' Titus gets up to shake Angad's hand. Victor and Idris follow, giving some space to the upset girls.

'Not at all,' Angad says smiling. 'What an asshole of a policeman …'

'Yeah!' Titus says with a shrug. 'Actually, they're the same everywhere—in my country too. Bloody goons, that's what they are. Anyway, congratulations on joining the army, man.'

'Thank you,' Angad smiles. 'And to you too, for Cornell. Well, nice meeting you. Enjoy your meal!'

'Yo—this is for you, my friend,' Victor calls out and Angad turns. Victor gives him a keychain. 'Come handy in army bootcamps, yo?'

Angad looks at a wrought-iron bottle-opener on a keychain, etched with the legend: 'Open your mind' on one side and 'African Students' Association' on the other. He flashes a smile at Victor and walks back to his table.

14

Khalid washes his hands and feet with water from a large plastic tank outside his garage. He shakes his hands dry and wraps a keffiyeh around his head. He squints through the haze at the distant minaret of the neighbourhood mosque and runs a hand over his crescent beard. The call for prayers should happen anytime now.

About a score of others are assembled around the garage. Khalid knows them all. Most of them are shopkeepers, vendors or labour from the locality. Several durries are spread out on the sidewalk and in the parking lane. Scooters and motorbikes have been parked to create a barricade against the traffic; the other vehicles are squeezing past the roadblock at a snail's pace.

'Khalid ustad,' Junaid walks up, rolling down the sleeves of his shirt. 'Should I go across to Mehra and ask him to lower the volume for now?'

He is a lanky young man, with hooded eyes and hollow cheeks giving him a perpetually hungry look. His tight, black jeans and baggy shirt are besmirched with grease and grime. He has a red-and-white keffiyeh draped around his vulturous neck with its prominent Adam's apple.

Khalid snorts in derision. 'You think that bastard will listen?'

'The azan will start soon, ustad. He can—'

'It's useless, Junaid,' Khalid cuts his apprentice short. 'We don't want to beg for our rights. If need be, we will snatch it with force, Inshallah! Have you fixed the horn on the Honda Activa?'

'I will do that right after the namaz, ustad,' Junaid says swiping the sweat from his brow.

'You have to be quicker,' Khalid growls. 'Unless you want a kick on your arse. I saw you gawking at those African whores and wasting time, you horny dog.'

'Can't help it, ustad,' Junaid grins. 'Those melon-like boobs, those tight buttocks ... I just want to tear their tight, short clothes and—'

'I know,' Khalid laughs. 'Those sluts are wild in bed. Last month, I was with one of them at a place near the university. Cost me ₹3,000 for an afternoon.'

Junaid starts to say something but Khalid stops him, and cranes his neck towards the mosque. He checks his watch with a frown. The bhajan playing from Mehra's speakers suddenly stops. A faint azan wafts across over the loudspeakers of the mosque. The men start to form lines, taking their positions on the durries.

15

Mehra watches as Bashir pulls the iron-grill gate of his restaurant and hangs a 'CLOSED' sign from the handle. He and his boys cross the road to join Khalid and the other men. Mehra checks his watch and ducks back into his shop.

'Sonu?' he calls out for one of his assistants. 'Is my stuff ready?'

'Yes, fa'ab,' Sonu lisps, opening the door of the mini fridge behind the cash counter. He takes out a bottle of Sprite and hands it to his employer. Mehra takes a big gulp and almost chokes.

'Idiot,' he splutters. 'How much vodka did you put into this bottle?'

'Fa'ab, I mikfed half-an-half,' Sonu replies, looking worried. 'If it too mild?'

'Mild?' Mehra screams and slaps Sonu. 'Is this mild? Moron. This is a bomb.'

'Fh-fhould I add fome water?'

'And ruin the fizz?' Mehra growls. 'No, I'll drink slowly. Did you load the recent bhajans in the new pen drive I brought? The special one?'

Sonu grins and nods vigorously.

'Ask the music guy to put that on,' Mehra says, looking out of the shop to where Bashir is talking to Khalid. He checks his watch and chuckles.

16

Bashir and Khalid slip off their sandals and stand together, ready to offer namaz. But right at that moment, a new bhajan explodes from Mehra's shop—a particularly noisy one with a clash of cymbals, loud drums and shrieking trumpets.

'Those motherfuckers are doing this deliberately,' Khalid tells Bashir. 'I shall just go and smash those speakers.'

'The azan has started,' Bashir lays a restraining hand on Khalid. 'It is time for namaz. We will deal with those lost souls later.'

'Your *later* never comes,' Khalid snaps. 'Even when they smashed the windscreen of your car.'

'We had no proof,' Bashir protests.

'Not when Mehra's men roughed up Junaid last month,' Khalid rants on. 'Not when you found a rack of pork ribs placed at the entrance of your restaurant …'

'Oye! I filed a police complaint!'

'And what good did that do?' Khalid spits out. 'Not even when that fat Bindal tried to molest Fatima. No—your *later* never comes. Why the fuck are you so scared?'

'*Scared*?' Bashir looks Khalid in the eye. 'I fought Russians when I was barely fourteen, killed two gun-wielding men in self-defence when I was twenty. You know that. I faced the horror and humiliation of prison for three years after that.

Did that break me? *Was* I scared? You think I don't face threats every day? Do I *tremble*? Do I *weep*? *Do I look fucking scared to you?*'

Khalid bridles but keeps quiet.

'I am not scared, you ass!' Bashir rumbles. 'I am smart. I use my head. I used my energy and resources to make my cousin a legislator. That is more useful than smashing up loudspeakers. I have faced more bullets than you have ever fired—asshole—and *survived* ... even prospered, I say. Don't you dare teach me how to be brave.'

Bashir kneels down with a grunt and closes his eyes. Khalid takes another look at Mehra's shop with clenched jaws, then kneels down too. He half-shuts his eyes, keeping a watch on the shop across.

17

Ali weaves through the crawling cars and two-wheelers and joins his sister waiting for him near Hari Shankar's cart, under a shady peepul tree.

Fatima quickly spreads out a couple of jute sacks on the hot stones of the sidewalk and makes her children sit down. Ali dumps his wares on the aluminium top of Hari Shankar's cart.

'I have sold four books and one packet of sketch pens so far, uncle,' he tells Hari Shankar proudly.

The ice cream vendor smiles and takes out an ice cream for Ali.

'After namaz, uncle,' Ali says, skipping over to his sister. Fatima greets him with a hug and ruffles his hair. They wash their hands and faces with some water from a bottle and stand next to each other, waiting for Khalid and his men to start the namaz across the street.

'This is not right,' Hari Shankar mutters.

'What's wrong?' Fatima looks up with a worried face. 'I—I can move away and do my namaz near that tree. I—'

'No, no, I didn't mean that, silly girl,' Hari Shankar waves his hands. 'I was talking about what Mehra is doing. He should turn off the loudspeakers for the namaz. It barely takes ten minutes. Listening to devotional songs should not be more important than actual prayers.'

'Why do you care, uncle?' Fatima grins with relief. 'You don't even worship the same God.'

Hari Shankar chuckles. 'I respected my parents. But that doesn't give me the cause to disrespect anyone else's—does it? I am sorry that noise is ruining your namaz today, my child.'

'Don't worry, uncle,' Fatima says, smiling. 'We don't stop namaz if a bird chirps or if we hear a thunderbolt. These are just songs. I like many of them. Come, Ali—let's kneel down for our prayers.'

18

Satpal props his elbows on the bonnet of the van. He flinches, scalded unexpectedly by the surface of the car, and draws away rubbing his skin. Placing a newspaper on the bonnet, he leans against it, puts on his sunglasses and looks around. Head Constable Gulshan is still dozing in his seat, hands resting on the steering wheel, snoring softly.

'It's a fucking furnace! Why is that fool not doing anything about this traffic?' Satpal asks Kultar, who's standing close by, swinging his cane.

'It won't clear up till those fellows finish their namaz,' Kultar observes in a flat voice, scratching his ear with his pinkie.

'Ask him to switch to manual control,' Satpal says, leaning into the PCR for a water bottle. He takes a long sip and throws the bottle back into the vehicle. The gesture doesn't wake up the aged constable. He watches Kultar walk across and instruct Amit, the traffic constable. They argue briefly till Kultar points back at Satpal. Amit nods and walks over to the control box below a lamppost.

'How can you sleep in this heat, Gulshan?' Satpal bangs at the door and pops his head into the cabin.

'Who says I am sleeping?' Gulshan mumbles with his eyes still shut.

'I could hear your damn snores,' Satpal says, grinning broadly at disrupting his old colleague's sleep, and takes his head out of the window. He leans against the car again with his back to Gulshan.

'Some fools believe everything they hear,' Gulshan says with a big yawn. 'I wasn't sleeping. I was dreaming.'

'Haha! Dreaming but not sleeping. Haha!' Satpal snorts. 'What wisdom, old man.'

'*Dream is not what you see in sleep. Dream is something that doesn't let you sleep,*' Gulshan sighs.

Satpal cocks an eyebrow and frowns. He turns around and pops his head back into the cabin. 'What did you say?'

'I didn't,' Gulshan yawns again and takes a big gulp of water from the bottle. 'Dr A.P.J. Abdul Kalam said it. Our late President.'

'Really?' Satpal asks. 'How do you know?'

'Because I read it,' Gulshan says, pulling out a crumpled paperback of *Ignited Minds* by Dr Kalam from under his bottom. 'Unlike some senior people.'

'Of course, I read,' Satpal says.

'Stupid tabloids and pornography don't count.' Gulshan shakes a finger at the sub-inspector.

'You used to be a schoolteacher in your village, isn't it?' Satpal asks after a moment of silence. 'Why did you join the police?'

Gulshan lights up a beedi and looks ahead. He takes a couple of deep puffs in silence. Satpal shakes his head and starts to pull out of the cabin.

'I guess, for the same reason as you. Wouldn't you say?' Gulshan says, blowing out a cloud of pungent smoke with a dry chuckle.

19

'Just forget him, Angad,' Thoi says. 'Most cops are uncouth bastards. No one knows that better than us.'

'Drunk on the power of the state,' Karl adds. 'It's the uniform that gives them that attitude.'

'A uniform does not give any attitude,' Angad snaps, clenching his teeth.

'Hey, it's not about you, buddy,' Raunak says, crunching a nacho. 'The bugger was probably jealous of you for being an army officer.'

'Yeah? And he was also jealous of me being a Sikh?' Angad asks, draining his glass of beer. Raunak quickly gestures at the waiter for another pitcher.

'Yeah, he must be *Sikh* to his *Gill* with your presence,' Partho, proud with his puns, says with a happy snort.

'If you throw your stupid puns one more time, I'm going to stab you with this fork,' Uma says, jabbing her fork at him.

'Oh, I wanna *fork*,' Partho goes on, snorting in glee. 'Will you *fork* me?'

Uma lunges at him and Karl pulls her back.

'You are bloody incorrigible,' she hisses. 'That policeman was harassing those foreign students. It was a violation of basic human rights. You think that's a joke?'

'You're not in America yet, where #*blacklivesmatter*, Uma,' Karl drawls. 'Get real. This is how the state subjugates us every day and you are only a witness to it.'

'Don't talk rubbish, Karl,' Uma snaps. 'Did you see how he behaved with Angad? And made fun of him because he's a Sikh? I *should* write about it on FB and X.'

'Oh, you saw that, did you?' Karl retorts. 'Did you see the same policeman speak to that poor woman selling flowers on the street? That one with the two kids?' Karl points at Fatima across the street. 'You can protest, write letters to editors, put it on social media or rant about it in your blog. But what about *that* poor woman? The bastard said his men *protected* her from getting raped. I bet it was *his* men who were trying to rape her. Where do the poor go in this country? Who do they turn to?'

'At least the rich can go abroad,' Partho quips.

20

Bindal stops at the ice cream cart and peers at the rate chart. He asks Hari Shankar for a Mango Dolly, then stands next to the cart, licking his ice cream and watching Fatima and Ali get ready to pray.

The young woman raises her hands to her chest and shuts her eyes. Bindal follows her movement and looks at her flimsy kameez. She is obviously not wearing a bra and the frayed fabric is revealing more than it is hiding. When Fatima bends forward to kneel, he catches a glimpse of her cleavage. He smirks.

'If you need new clothes, come to my shop any evening, after business hours,' he tells Fatima. 'I like to help the poor, understand?'

Fatima ignores Bindal and bows her head to the ground. Hari Shankar looks worried and edges between them, to hide her from the man's lecherous looks.

'S-sir, they are praying,' he informs, half pleading, half warning.

Bindal laughs and bites into his ice cream. With lingering steps, he walks around Fatima and Ali and stands looking at her.

'Is your ice cream licence up to date?' he asks Hari Shankar.

'Oh yes, sir.'

'That boy also sells pirated books for you,' Bindal continues. 'It is illegal, understand?'

Hari Shankar looks on helplessly.

21

'I should have punched the motherfucker,' Victor says, taking a deep swallow of beer.

'Hey, it's over. We've discussed this enough,' Titus says. 'Those guys were just looking to make some quick money from foreigners. Luckily that army guy interfered today. Must have pissed off the cop.'

'You could have called your embassy and complained. You know everyone there,' Sharon says. 'That was harassment.'

'Yeah? And say what?' Titus asks. 'That a policeman was asking to check our documents? He is authorized to do that. We only bring in the embassy as a last resort. As the general secretary of the African Students' Association, I cannot antagonize the local police unnecessarily. This was no big deal.'

'He called us "sluts",' Faith whispers. 'I guess that's no big deal for you guys.'

Titus stiffens and looks at Victor and then at Idris. They both look down. Sharon reaches out and holds Faith's hands.

'I guess if he strip-searched me here, it wouldn't be a *big deal* either,' Faith continues in a flat tone.

'Hey, Faith! Now look—' Victor protests.

'No, *you* look, Victor.' Faith has tears in her eyes. 'I never told you guys about what happened to me last weekend. The landlord's son had come home to collect rent. I was having a beer and writing my dissertation. I offered him a can and he accepted. The next thing I knew ... he ... he was trying to kiss me. I ... I ...'

'Why didn't you tell me anything?' Titus asks, reaching out to Faith.

'And risk being thrown out of my PG?' Faith asks, looking up at Titus. 'Or risk being told that it's *no big deal?*'

22

Namaz over, they all stand up. Some start folding away the durries. Bashir walks over to the plastic water tank and splashes some water on his face. Khalid offers a hand towel. As Bashir pats his face dry, Khalid looks towards Mehra's shop. A table is being laid out for their feast.

'This can't go on,' Khalid hisses at Bashir, who quietly folds the towel and hands it back.

'Khan Chacha,' Junaid says, walking up. 'You need to do something about that Mehra. *We* want to do something.'

Bashir wears his sandals and stands looking at them without uttering a word.

'Why can't we just walk over and smash the damn loudspeakers? It may help.'

'And *then* what?' Bashir asks calmly, taking a small silver box of cardamoms out of his pockets and popping one in his mouth. He offers the box around. A small crowd of the faithful has gathered around them by now.

'That is a deliberate act to disrupt our prayers,' Khalid fumes.

'So you will destroy property and go to jail?' Bashir asks. 'You see that police fellow Satpal? He is itching to have a go at us. He only keeps quiet because he knows my cousin is a legislator. But if we give him a chance—he's going to screw us.'

'So we won't do anything?' Junaid asks, angrily. 'Are we like weak and stupid women?'

'You *really* think women are weak and stupid, do you? Then you need to get married, Junaid,' Bashir says with a crooked smile. 'No, we wait for the right moment. We will burn Mehra's shop down when the opportunity arises. And, also, his arse-licker, Bindal's.'

23

'I think that traffic cop is trying to do something to clear this mess,' Suraj says, his eyes following Amit as he makes his way to the signal control panel.

'Do you think we can catch the suppliers before they shut for lunch?' Lorna asks of Malaika.

'I'll just give them a call.'

Malaika makes the call.

'They say they will wait for us,' she says with a sigh of relief. 'Hurry up, Suraj! Want me to take over the wheel?'

Suraj bristles and honks a few times. There is hardly any movement of the vehicles ahead of them. He bangs his palms on the steering wheel.

'You see those autos ahead, the ones parked next to the ice cream cart?' Suraj says over his shoulder. 'They are blocking the damned incoming lane. All those bastards come from villages and then create a mess in this town. And those other buggers doing namaz have blocked the lane on our side after the signal.'

'I really want ice cream,' Lorna wails like a child. 'Should I get it myself?'

'I think the traffic will clear up in a moment,' Priscilla says. 'We'll just pull up next to the cart and buy you one. It's too hot and dusty outside.'

'We can't just pull up there, it's on the wrong side of the street,' Lorna protests.

'Relax,' Malaika drawls, rolling down her window and lighting up another cigarette. 'We are in a big imported car and this is India. It doesn't matter on which side we stop. At least we're not driving over people sleeping on pavements. That traffic cop is bloody useless. And these damn jaywalkers are all over the place. Gosh! At times I feel like actually mowing them all down.'

'Jesus! Malaika, calm down,' Lorna says, shaking her head with exasperation. 'They are humans and your countrymen.'

'They are just parasites!'

24

Bindal's cell phone rings. He quickly finishes his ice cream and throws the stick down. Hari Shankar picks it up and puts it away in the waste-carton.

'Mehra sa'ab?' Bindal answers the phone. 'Yes, I'm just round the corner ... no, no, just two minutes away. Oh? Chilled, is it? I'm coming over.' He casts one last smirk at Fatima and walks away. Fatima's eyes follow Bindal's receding back, his fat arms swinging and feet wobbling over the road. She gets up, folds the quilted rag she uses as a prayer mat and stuffs it into her jute shoulder bag. Her eyes are pink and moist.

'Ammi?' Murad whimpers, reaching out. Fatima looks down at her son for a moment, her lips quivering. With a sigh, she smiles and picks up the child, who wraps his matchstick legs around her waist. His older sister, Nafisa, frowns and snuggles closer to her mother.

25

Traffic Constable Amit pulls open the traffic control panel and inserts his key. He turns it off and looks at the traffic lights to check. He shuts the panel and hurries to the crossing. Spotting the two autos, he marches down, frowning, and screams at the drivers.

Ramji listens without any expression, then points at a small sign saying 'AUTO STAND'. The policeman glares back till Ramji looks away and lights up a smoke.

The cacophony of horns is now deafening and Amit rushes to the crossing blowing his whistle, shouting and waving his arms around. He manages to create a small clearing for traffic coming in from the side of Khan Khana Restaurant and notes with relief that Khalid's men are getting back to their shops.

The big, black SUV is honking like the sound itself would blast the traffic away. Amit waves at the driver with angry gestures asking him to stop the racket, then turns away to open the cross traffic, with a little smile of satisfaction on his face. The SUV remains stuck.

26

Hari Shankar gives an ice cream to Ali, who accepts it and offers it to Fatima's daughter. He laughs and takes out two more for Ali and Fatima. The toddler tries to reach out for one, but Hari Shankar shakes his head with a smile.

'You're doing very well, Ali,' Hari Shankar says, patting the boy. 'Your brother earned 120 rupees yesterday,' he tells Fatima. She nods with a smile and attempts to pay for the ice cream but Hari Shankar refuses.

'Has that man Bindal been troubling you?' he asks.

Fatima squats down next to her baby boy and says nothing. Her face is inscrutable. She lets the infant take a few licks of the cream. He gets the syrup all over his face and she wipes it with a piece of cloth.

'If he is, you should let me know,' Hari Shankar offers. 'Just because we are poor doesn't mean we—'

'Why?' Fatima snaps. Her lips quiver and her eyelashes flutter down to cage in the welling moistness at the corners.

'Why, what?'

'What can you do?' Fatima lashes out. 'I heard Bindal threaten you about selling these books. He can stop that. Whatever Ali is earning will stop. Why should I tell you anything?'

'Well ... I could ...' Hari Shankar stammers, taken aback by the young woman's anger.

'Yes,' Ramji comes to his friend's aid. 'We may be poor but not helpless. I know people in our Union who—'

'Who will take up a fight for a street woman?' Fatima lashes out at Ramji. 'Who won't be bothered by my religion, my class or my situation? Who will not ask me to get into their bed in return for protection?'

Ali watches his sister's outburst silently and eats his ice cream. The flies buzzing around the stick don't bother him even when they squat down on the food. He just blows them off.

'You are a good man, Hari Kaka,' Fatima says, finishing her ice cream and throwing the stick in the trash box. She wipes her eyes with the back of her hand. 'But you cannot help me. You cannot even help *yourself*. We are meant to crawl on the streets while we live—get kicked, trampled, abused. And when we die, our bodies are taken away to be burned like dead dogs. That big, black car can run over me and my children right now and *nothing* will happen to the people inside. *Nothing!* Do you understand? *Nothing!* I've seen it all.'

'Fatima, child,' Hari Shankar shakes his head with a look of pained compassion. 'You have to look at the positives ... you have children. The Almighty can—'

'If He can *do* anything,' Fatima screams, 'let Him take away this hole between my legs—the reason for my misery and suffering!' She pounds her thighs with her fists and there is nothing anyone does to stop her.

27

Amit observes that the cross traffic has more or less cleared up and the traffic on the main street is getting longer. With a sigh, he returns to the control panel and flips a switch that puts the signal system back on automatic. He can almost sense the sub-inspector glaring at him for doing it, so he keeps his back turned to his senior.

Amit removes his cap and wipes his sweaty forehead and hair, which is gritty with dust. Forcing himself to keep his back facing the parked police vehicle, he walks crablike down the sidewalk to the ice cream cart. An oncoming Bindal bumps into him.

'Are you blind?' Bindal asks, enraged.

'Watch where you are going, fatso,' Amit retorts.

'You better talk nicely to me, understand?' Bindal says.

'Or else? Do you own this street?'

'Bloody traffic constable—you think you're the boss around here?' Bindal barks.

'Your new car is parked in that back street, no?' Amit says. 'Think I haven't seen it? That's no-parking zone. Want it towed away?'

'Touch it and see what will happen to you, asshole! Understand?'

28

Mehra can see Bindal arguing with the traffic cop, his arms flailing. He sighs and takes another large swig from his bottle. He squeezes his eyes shut and swallows hard as he opens them, then shakes his head with a grimace.

He turns his gaze to Bashir and his gang standing near Khalid's garage, glaring at him. Mehra sniggers and walks over to the two men sitting by the amplifier. He leans forward to peer at the controls, finds the volume control and tweaks it a notch or two higher. He puts down his bottle on the table.

He starts to jauntily strut up and down the pavement, breaking into a small jig every now and then. From the corner of his eyes, he sees shoppers, passers-by and shopkeepers looking at him. But that does not stop him from gloating.

He whirls around and heads to his shop, aware of the dark looks from Khalid and his men across the street. He half-shuts his eyes and folds his hands, snapping the fingertips together in rhythm with the music, and then breaking into an impromptu dance once again, only to taunt them, before ducking into his shop.

29

Suraj sees the brake lights of the car ahead of him turn off as it starts to crawl ahead.

'Still want that ice cream?' he asks, half-turning.

'Yes, puh-leez,' Lorna begs.

Suraj inches to his right, trying to cut across to the other side of the street before the oncoming cars block the big gap that has formed between the two lanes. Finding his left clear of the car ahead, he steers sharply and pumps the accelerator pedal, to get close to the cart. The car ahead of him breaks all of a sudden and a hand sticks out to wave at someone on the pavement.

30

Ali hugs Fatima and she ruffles his hair. He smiles and picks up his bundle of books and pens. The signal turns green and the line of vehicles starts creeping ahead.

A car stops abruptly in front of the cart, and the man inside rolls down his window to wave at him. Ali grins. He recognizes the car and the driver. A regular customer.

Ali grabs his bundle and dashes across the street.

31

Suraj swerves further to the right to avoid the rear bumper of the car ahead and curses loudly. He straightens the steering, making the SUV lurch towards the opposite sidewalk, then cuts sharply to his left to align his side to the pavement. From the corner of his eye, he sees the boy approaching the curb waving a handful of pirated books in the air. He slams the brake immediately but it's too late—the bonnet ploughs into the boy! There is a dull thud, and the boy drops down, out of sight. The car bumps over something and the women around him scream as the SUV shudders to a stop.

32

Bindal stops mid-sentence with his mouth half-open and stares over Amit's shoulders.

'What? Your jaws got tired, fatso?' Amit asks. 'Yes, I do have videos of what you do in your shop's basement after your boys leave at night. There is a ventilator at street level you forgot about. Every young beggar girl in the area is sick of you. And last Saturday …? You disgusting bastard—the older one is only fourteen years old! Should I take the video to Satpal?'

Bindal is in a trance and doesn't utter a word. His eyes look glazed over.

'What? You thought no one knew? And do you think no one knows about the stock of kerosene you sell on the sly? I have photos of the delivery vans and your boys carrying them inside. Civil supplies inspectors will love those too. No words coming out anymore, is it now? You filthy pervert.'

'Asshole,' Bindal finally speaks, his voice low. 'Look behind you, dimwit!'

Amit turns around and freezes.

33

Satpal hears the screeching noise and loud crash, and looks up. From where he stands, his view is blocked by the line of vehicles, but he can see Hari Shankar and Fatima.

They are standing with shocked expressions, staring at something below Satpal's line of sight. The two auto drivers slowly take a few wary steps towards the SUV. There is a sudden lull in the incessant honking as vehicles fall silent. All the pedestrians seem to have frozen in their tracks and are looking at the spot on the street next to the SUV.

Satpal turns his head and surveys the street. A little down the pavement, Amit and Bindal are also staring in the direction of the SUV, which itself seems unharmed. The people inside are sitting very still.

'Kultar,' Satpal calls out to the constable. 'Go and have a look. Is it an accident?'

34

'And do you know what that Bindal truly is?' Khalid asks Bashir. 'He is a fiend. The things he does …'

'One day We shall seize you with a mighty onslaught: We will indeed then exact Retribution!' Bashir says quietly. 'Surah Ad-Dukhan. Patience!'

All of a sudden, traffic has come to a standstill and the horns have stopped. Only the cacophony from Mehra's loudspeakers fills up the street.

People are turning towards the black SUV near Hari Shankar's cart. Khalid cranes his neck to look over the roofs of cars. He gets a glimpse of Hari Shankar and Fatima staring at something on the street. Across the street, Bindal and the traffic constable are also looking towards the same spot.

'Junaid!' Khalid calls for his apprentice, urgently.

'Ustad?' The strapping youngster comes running out of the garage.

'—Fatima seems to be in some trouble,' Khalid says. 'Take a couple of boys and find out what happened.'

35

From across the street, Mehra sees Khalid give instructions to his boys. His eyes narrow as four of them, led by Junaid, march off towards the spot. Mehra takes a long gulp from his bottle and calls out to his shop assistants. They don't hear him above the din of the loudspeakers, so he walks up to the shopfront and lets out a stream of expletives. Sonu and Veeru come scampering out.

'Khalid is sending some of his boys over there,' Mehra says, pointing towards the SUV. 'It must be a ploy to start trouble and ruin our puja. Go and find out what they are up to.'

He sees Kultar rush to the spot too. Satpal seems to be relaxed, though looking on curiously.

Mehra sees Bashir patting Khalid on his chest, trying to calm the younger man down. Khalid jabs a finger at the loudspeakers. Mehra takes another large swig, pulls out his cell phone and punches out a number.

'Gidwani?' he says, walking into his shop. 'I think that conniving swine Bashir and his dog Khalid are trying to create trouble. Call all our people in the market and ask them to get ready to respond if those bastards do anything. Put Monty in charge right now. What? No ... not yet. Today, if they try anything, we must show them our muscle. This market cannot have two lions ... Yes, and then hurry to my shop—and remember to carry your pistol. I'm glad we prepared for this eventuality yesterday. Tell your men to get ready for a showdown.'

Mehra enters his little cubicle inside the shop and unlocks a steel almirah. He takes out a .32 IOF Ashani pistol and checks the magazine—it is fully loaded with eight bullets. He slips it into the pocket of his loose kurta and walks out to the street.

36

Ali lies face down on the street, his legs splayed out. His left arm is stretched in line with his shoulder and his right is twisted under his still body at an impossible angle. There is a dark patch of crimson forming under his right cheek which is pressed to the gravelly bitumen. His eyes are shut. The bundle of pirated books lie crushed under the front wheels of the SUV and his colourful packets of sketch pens are scattered everywhere.

Deepak halts and squats a couple of feet away from Ali, scared to go closer. He reaches out a hand to touch the boy but draws it back to look up at Ramji, who in turn looks at Fatima and back at Hari Shankar. In a daze, he picks up a few packets of sketch pens and walks back to hand them over to Hari Shankar who drops them, instinctively, in his trash box.

Fatima is gasping loudly, making low, whimpering noises between occasional loud sobs.

Amit, the traffic constable, reaches the spot huffing and puffing. Bindal almost bumps into him from behind. From up the street, Junaid and his friends come racing down. Shortly, Constable Kultar skirts the SUV and joins the small crowd of onlookers. They all stare at Ali's body in glum silence.

'Is he dead?' Kultar asks, looking around. Fatima lets out a piercing scream.

37

'Do you think we should order some more appetizers?' Bonium asks, interrupting Karl and waving at a waiter.

Angad grins at the teenager and claps him on the shoulder. 'I like your diet, man.'

'I don't mind something vegetarian,' Uma announces. 'So, Karl, what is the solution to this issue? Should Angad accept what that inspector said and keep quiet? Because that man saved the poor woman once?'

'No, but we can stop and see the problem from all angles. We can take a step back to understand why it really happened. Why—'

'Because he is an asshole and a bigot!' Uma says, firmly.

'You are talking about the symptoms, Uma. I am asking you to recognize the disease.'

'What disease?'

'Anger and poverty—the root causes of the problems. Poverty feeds anger. Do we know how many people live below the poverty line? What challenges they have to face on a daily basis? The number of poor people in the country society comes up many times is staggering. They have to fight for even the most basic needs. Obviously, they will be angry. Angry with the world, with us. Thus, society, as a whole is becoming angrier. I believe that it is anger that makes that inspector a bigot, that makes you react to—'

'What you are essentially saying is that as a society we are becoming angrier and that poverty is the cause of that anger? You think I don't know the reality of the world? Just because I am privileged, will I be blind to everything around me?'

'No, Uma, that's not what I said. There is a huge gap in society, created by poverty and fed by anger. This poverty—'

'Yes, blame poverty for all the problems, and treat it as an excuse!'

'I don't blame everything on poverty,' Karl retorts. 'I was only making an observation. We, the people of this country, are angry because we're poor and poor because we are angry. The GDP seems to be on the rise, but not everyone is benefitting. People are getting left out, and not included in this so-called *growth*. Coming back to that policeman …'

Uma and Partho groan in unison.

'Yeah, right,' Uma sneers. 'You will say that the asshole is a product of poverty?'

'In a way, yes,' Karl says, sipping at his beer. 'Most likely, he comes from a family much poorer than any of ours. Good education costs money, Uma. That education helps you get better jobs—makes you an army officer or … an adman, or even a journalist like me. It definitely enables some people to go to the US for higher education.'

'Come to your damn point,' Uma interjects, shaking her head in irritation.

'What do you think went through his mind when he came into this pub? When he saw a bunch of college kids sitting in air-conditioned luxury, while he has to stand out in the heat every day? When he saw us sipping imported beer? What did he feel when he saw pretty girls like you all—'

'Thank you,' Thoi giggles.

'—pretty girls, who he knows will never look at him because he is beneath their economic strata?' Karl continues, ignoring her. 'How would he feel when he sees those African students celebrating, when he was probably taught that the darker you are, the more inferior you are? Or that his caste places him higher in society than some people and beneath others? Or when he sees our Raunak wearing a heavy gold chain, weighing a kilo?'

Uma shrugs and looks at others. Some in the group listen intently and some sit with their heads down.

'*It makes him angry!*' Karl supplies the answer, thumping the table.

'I get angry too,' Thoi says, quietly. 'Sometimes people here make me feel like a freak in my own country. The people in our state are well-to-do, but don't enjoy all the facilities available here. And people are aware of this difference. They do not leave any stone unturned to remind me of my place. So, yes, I am angry.'

'See? Now can you say that this divide or xenophobia can be blamed on poverty?' Uma challenges Karl. Angad groans and hangs his head.

'The pie may be getting bigger, but the portion for everyone is still limited,' Karl says, after a pause. Uma rolls her big eyes. 'Everyone wants a piece of the same pie. It's like *Fight Club* for survival. The pie is sliced from all angles—from left to right, top to bottom, inside and outside. So, some people decide to draw lines and break down the world into segments—on the basis of region, religion, colour, race, caste, nationality. Make everything "us versus them" and put them in a field to fight it out. Eliminate as many "other" groups as possible and limit the competition within your own group. The size of the pie remains the same. But now everyone can have a bite, everyone in your own group. So, keep as many people away from it as you can. Keep Northeasterners away by making their lives difficult so they go back to where they came from. Obviously, the "outsider" will face a similar situation there.'

'I don't quite buy your theory, dude,' Partho says. 'That poor-angry-poor cycle doesn't make sense. Income levels have risen a lot in the past few years, and life is becoming better. People are earning more, spending more. It really depends on what people, individuals that is, make of themselves—'

'And yet we see an unnerving increase in random violence,' Karl says, leaning forward. 'Not just minor incidents—it is brutal gang rapes with mutilation and murder, people shooting and killing in instances of petty road rage, mob violence, arson, destruction and mayhem. Constantly fighting for a slice of the pie makes people perpetually angry. These inhibit their ability to come together, work side-by-side, build something and take the country forward. And this in turn leads to no development. Which causes more anger and …' He falls silent and shrugs.

Uma gazes at Karl for a long time and lets out a sigh. 'Know what?' she says. 'Whatever your theory is, you are doing a bad job of explaining it. You are not making any sense, Mr Journalist, and are talking shit.'

'Hey, hey!' Angad intervenes. 'Let's not get so personal here. We have all known each other for so long ... Let's order some food. Where's that damn waiter?' He waves at the waiter who is busy serving another table and raises two fingers, seeking a couple of minutes.

'Look, I have now been a reporter for almost a year,' Karl says. 'Been to different parts of this country, met people, seen the beauty and ugliness of our land and people. I can tell you one thing—there is a lot of anger everywhere. It is a tinder box. The only explanation I have is we are a society of extreme paucity. There is just too much deprivation, too much denial ... there is just too little of everything. That breeds discontent and irrepressible anger in people. Anything can ignite us, start a fire so bad that it will burn everything in its path. We don't really need a reason. Often, people don't even know why they are so angry.'

'What is that supposed to mean?' Uma persists. 'There is always a cause ... like some provocation. It's not just a subconscious reaction to deprivation.'

'This country is full of street dogs and, sometimes, people get bitten,' Karl says, wagging a finger. 'Yet, one fine day, people go berserk after street dogs bite a man and they burn down buses. Trains run late. But, for some strange reason, one special day, passengers start stoning trains, torching stations. Many places have a shortage of drinking water, but inexplicably, on a particular day, a crowd goes on a rampage, pelts the police with stones, vandalizes shops, destroys property. And no one can later tell who started it or why on that day. Why?'

'There could be many explanations,' Uma bridles, flicking strands of hair away from her face. She looks around, seeking support from others. No one speaks.

'Do you have any other explanation than pent-up fury?' Karl asks quietly. 'And what could be a common cause for that fury—if not paucity and deprivation and denial? In short, poverty.'

'Um—there is mob violence and arson in developed countries too, you know?' Partho says.

'Didn't I say the size of the pie is limited everywhere?' Karl retorts. 'There are always the angry marginalized.'

The waiter comes towards the table, smiling, and stands with an e-tablet in his hand. 'Yes sir? Can I take your order?'

Bonium grabs the menu and reads it intently.

'Um … one crispy vegetable, one tandoori mushroom, one … no, make it two plates of—' He looks at the waiter to see him not paying any attention to him, but looking outside… 'Hello? Excuse me?'

Angad looks up and follows the waiter's gaze. Across the street, the Audi Q7 is standing at the wrong spot, turned towards the opposite lane. A small crowd has gathered around it. The flower girl the policeman had earlier pointed to is standing near the car, sobbing.

38

Constable Kultar kneels down next to Deepak and observes Ali. He checks for the boy's pulse.

'He is alive!' Kultar announces over his shoulder.

There is an audible sigh of relief all around, but Fatima continues sobbing. Hari Shankar talks softly to her daughter and makes the child sit down under the peepul tree with her baby brother. He walks over and tries to calm Fatima down.

The circle of people slowly edges in towards Ali. Kultar waves his cane and wards them off.

'Stay away. This is an accident site,' he warns. 'Do not come close or touch anything. We don't know if this boy will survive.'

Kultar gently turns Ali over with Deepak's help and inspects the wound. He pulls out a grubby handkerchief and dabs at Ali's nose and ears. He hands over the handkerchief to Deepak and takes out his cell phone.

39

Satpal listens to the report over the phone, his face scrunched in irritation. He grunts out monosyllabic responses as Kultar fills him in. He casts a sidelong glance at Head Constable Gulshan sitting behind the steering and pulls a face. *There will be no lunch break today,* he mouths.

'No, I don't want to come down as yet,' Satpal barks into the phone. 'I am trying to call an ambulance. Till then, handle the situation over there. It's just an accident involving a street boy, so no big deal. But I can see Khalid's and Mehra's men rushing around. We can expect trouble, so be alert. Get all the people in the car to our van. Taking statements from them might be difficult there. Hopefully, the boy lives and we can help strike a deal between Fatima and the car's owner. Keep that Amit by your side. What …? Screw the traffic for now. There's nothing he can do. People won't or can't move—it's a mess for us and free entertainment for the crowd.'

Satpal disconnects the call and asks Gulshan to report the accident to the control room on the wireless and requisition an ambulance.

40

Suraj is unable to move and clutches fiercely at the padded steering wheel. He shifts his eye to see what the policeman and the other man are doing but they are not in his line of sight.

'Go out and check what happened, Suraj!' Priscilla whispers. 'I think you hit someone …'

'We were barely crawling,' Lorna adds from the back seat. 'How did this happen? It can't be so bad, right? I mean the car could have hit the pavement. Oh! There is a cop here. We are safe. He will do something—'

'Safe?' says Malaika. 'Lorna, you have no idea! Do you see that crowd of lowlives? They just need any excuse to lynch us!'

'What?' Lorna exclaims. 'Why? Suraj didn't do it deliberately. Someone just jumped in front of our car. Why would they do anything to us?'

Malaika looks Lorna in the eyes. 'Because, Mademoiselle Lorna from Brussels, we are the crème -de-la-crème of society. They would want money—'

'Don't be ridiculous!' Lorna shakes her head in disbelief. 'Acc-accidents happen. There is a procedure to handle that. There is the law. We *do* have a uniformed policeman out there. Su-Suraj will be fine.'

'The policeman?' Malaika asks. 'You think he will be on our side?'

'Hell—no!' Lorna exclaims with a shocked expression. 'He will be on the side of the law.'

'Lorna, you and I,' Malaika tries to be calm. 'Are the *haves*. Those beggars, policemen... the crowd out there are *have-nots*. They are *all on the same bloody side*. Against us!'

'Go on, Suraj!' Lorna says. 'We cannot just keep sitting in here.'

'Do *not* unlock the fuckin' door,' Malaika screams. 'Can you take a U-turn and make a run? Get us out of here first.'

'*Are you crazy?*' Lorna is dumbfounded.

'No, *they* are,' Malaika points at the people gathering at the spot.

'There is no space for us to turn the car,' Suraj says, his voice shaking a little.

The policeman straightens and they can see him from the windshield now. He takes out a pocket notebook, bends to check the licence plate and carefully jots it down. He waves the crowd away from the car, strides up to the driver's window and peeks in. He taps on the window with his cane and gestures at Suraj to roll the glass down.

41

Khalid and Bashir listen to Aslam, one of the boys who'd been sent with Junaid to find out what was happening. Khalid recites a quick prayer of gratitude when Aslam informs them that Ali is alive.

'Inshallah, the boy will be okay,' Bashir says. 'I will call for the Wakf Council ambulance. We must take care of our own. Any idea about the people in the car?'

'The driver has a big tika on his forehead,' Aslam replies with a meaningful look. 'There are three women in the car. One African, one ... maybe Chinese ... and a local. Rich people.'

'I will make them pay dearly for this,' Khalid growls. 'I will smash—'

'Khalid, Khalid ...' Bashir says placing a hand on Khalid's shoulder. 'Smashing, burning, slashing ... is not always the right solution.'

'But—'

'However, a situation like this can give us an excuse to do all that. Those unfortunate people in the car are no good for us. They will possibly try to pay their way out of this. But you're right, we should protect our own. Ali's accident ... it may be a good opportunity to do something more meaningful ... to that arrogant Mehra ... and Bindal ...'

Khalid looks at Bashir with a puzzled frown. He looks over at Mehra, who is staring back at them from across the street. The two hold their gaze for a few moments. With a slow, deliberate motion, Mehra pulls out a pistol from his pocket. He pretends to check it, and then puts it back in his pocket. Giving a lopsided smile to Khalid, he turns to pay attention to the accident spot.

42

Beggars, roadside vendors, passers-by and labourers from every street corner have swarmed to the spot. They jostle for a better view of Ali's injured body and the drama unfolding between the police constable and the rich folks.

A few women beggars who know Fatima ensconce her in a protective circle. They caress and embrace their wailing sister, while casting dark looks at the passengers in the car.

Bindal watches them from a distance, licking his pendulous lips. His eyes dart around, assessing the growing crowd. He starts taking small, slow steps backwards—squeezing past unrelenting bodies, sliding through narrow gaps in the human wall forming around him. But then he steps on someone's toes and stops dead.

Firm hands grab his shoulders and turn him around. He confronts a small group of construction workers, their faces ghostly white under coats of cement dust and flecks of plaster-of-Paris. Bindal notices a man wearing a talisman disc with ہللا, an Arabic inscription, on it and curses under his breath. He is nervous and takes a step to move past them.

Another dust-covered hand slides through the human mass and strikes him playfully on his face. Bindal gasps and covers his cheeks with his hands. Several hands sprout around him and feel his gold chain, claw his bejewelled fingers and tug at his silk kurta. Bindal feels his pyjamas getting wet. He looks down in horror to find a dark, wet patch forming on the hem of his kurta. He hears derisive laughter around him and cowers.

All of a sudden, the men part and offer a narrow channel of escape. Bindal looks about with suspicion but the inscrutable, dust-caked faces are not looking at him anymore. He starts an awkward, sideways shuffle through the gap and comes out of the crowd, sobbing with relief.

There is a sudden, sharp tug at the back of his collar as a gnarled fist grabs it from behind. Bindal tries to move but the hand holds on tight till the fabric tears with a loud, ripping sound. The hand lets go and Bindal runs, the torn strip of his kurta fluttering behind him like a limp orange flag.

43

Back at the car, Constable Kultar waves his cane, asking Suraj to lower his window. As soon as Suraj's face is seen, Kultar demands to see his driving licence. In a daze, and sweating profusely, Suraj hands it over. Kultar pockets Suraj's driving licence and turns his attention to the two ladies sitting in the rear seat. He moves down to Malaika's window and taps on the glass with his cane. She lowers it.

'Is this your car, madam?' he asks. Behind him, he can sense the crowd getting excited.

'Yes—no,' Malaika fumbles. Kultar glares at her.

'I mean,' she says, stammering. 'It is registered in the name of my company, Indic Fibres Private Limited.' She offers a visiting card.

'Papers?' Kultar asks, dropping the visiting card into his shirt pocket. He turns around and beckons Amit.

'In the glove compartment,' Malaika says, mustering up the confidence to keep her voice calm. 'And the insurance has been recently renewed. And the pollution certificate. All are in the glove compartment.'

'Your car ran over a boy, madam,' Kultar says, flipping open his notebook. 'Your name, phone number and address?'

'Look, it was an accident,' Malaika reasons. 'The boy jumped in front of the car from nowhere.'

Kultar takes a step back and looks at the car. He turns to Amit for support.

'Madam, this car is on the wrong side of the street,' Amit chips in. 'That is a traffic violation. It is rash and negligent driving under Section 279 of the IPC.'

'Suraj is the assistant vice-president of my company,' Malaika explains hurriedly. Kultar looks on with a blank expression. 'Suraj had followed the car ahead of us, but that idiot braked suddenly. Suraj had to turn right to avoid a collision. That's when the boy jumped in front of the car and …'

'And now he is lying in a pool of blood,' Kultar says dryly. 'Just because you own a big, imported car doesn't mean you own the road, madam.'

Malaika looks sideways at Lorna who lowers her eyes. Malaika takes a few deep breaths and takes out her phone.

'No calls, madam,' Kultar swiftly takes Malaika's phone away. 'This is a serious accident. The boy may die. Step out please.'

'I was trying to call an ambulance,' Malaika snaps, but sobers down immediately. 'I-I just want to help the boy. Please let me make the call.'

'Step out of the car, madam,' Kultar orders, his voice shaking. 'We need to check if any of you is under the influence of liquor or drugs.'

'What?' Malaika asks, her lips curled. 'This is an accident. Why are you harassing us? Do not try to harass us.' She tries to roll up her window, but Kultar sticks his cane in the small gap.

Amit takes this opportunity to remove the ignition key from its slot.

'Come out of the car,' Kultar repeats. 'You are obstructing the police now.'

'We will take the boy to—'

'Madam, we have already called an ambulance,' Kultar informs. 'You have to come with me to the PCR vehicle parked ahead and meet the sub-inspector.'

'We are not getting out of this car,' Malaika says. 'I know the racket you policemen run with these urchins and beggars. We will drive straight to the police station where we will talk in the presence of our lawyer. Priscilla, call up Advocate Kapil Ahuja and tell him about the incident. Ask him to reach the station immediately.'

Kultar glares at Malaika but can do nothing as Priscilla makes a quick phone call. He yanks open the driver's door and asks Suraj to step out.

44

'Looks like there's been an accident,' Karl observes. 'Another story of a big SUV mowing down some pavement dweller, you think? I'll just have a look.'

'The police are there,' Uma says. 'You don't have to poke your nose—'

'Damn it! I am a reporter, Uma,' Karl snaps.

'I-I think we should all wait here,' Thoi says. 'Let's just finish our lunch and leave. I have a bad feeling about all this. Please?'

'Yeah man, probably no big story for you there,' Partho drawls. 'The police will take both parties aside, money will change hands and that's it. This is no breaking-news stuff. Relax!'

'Partho is right, Karl,' Angad says, patting Karl's arm. 'That's just everyday stuff. Not worth your while.'

Karl sighs and settles back, sipping his beer. Out on the street, the policeman is arguing with the passengers in the SUV.

45

'I'm concerned about what Mehra is plotting now,' Bashir says. 'Why was he showing off his gun to us?'

'We have guns too, Khan Chacha,' Khalid bristles. 'I will show him that!'

'You will show nothing,' Bashir says, with a touch of irritation. 'In a game of cards, you don't reveal your hand early. Learn to think smart. Do you have the petrol bottles ready?'

'Yes, Khan Chacha,' Aslam says. 'Khalid Bhai has given that job to me. I keep fifty bottles, ready and stocked, in the storage area inside. I check on them every week.'

'Good, good,' Bashir says, nodding slowly. 'How many guns are here right now?'

'I have my pistol in my desk,' Khalid says. 'I know Junaid keeps his country-made gun in the toolbox of his motorbike. And of course, Salim Bhai there carries his revolver—it's a licensed one.'

'We know Mehra has about forty shopkeepers of this market in his gang,' Bashir says. 'I think he is up to something. We should be prepared.'

'There are eighteen of us here already, Khan Chacha,' Khalid says, looking around at the namaz assembly. 'And about ten more are in the nearby market area. They don't attend the namaz regularly, but they are with us. I trust them.'

'Okay, give them a call and ask them to be on alert,' Bashir says. 'If the right opportunity arises today, we will teach this Mehra and his rabid friends a lesson they won't forget. But remember, we wait till Mehra reveals his plan.'

46

'How did this happen?' Mehra asks Bindal.

'I ... I was there when the accident happened, understand?' Bindal replies, taking a big gulp from Mehra's bottle. 'Then a group of workers started pushing and shoving me. Someone even slapped me. And when I tried to leave, someone tore my kurta.'

Bindal's shop assistant Punit comes forward with a new set of kurta-pyjamas. Mehra watches with a bemused expression as Bindal changes right there in the middle of the shop. The thick tyres of flab around his belly glisten with sweat. He dumps his soggy and torn clothes into a polythene bag that Punit carries away.

'Did you recognize anyone?'

Bindal takes another long swig, looking across the street at Bashir and Khalid, who were looking back at him.

'No, but they were ... they were from *their* side,' Bindal says, pointing across the lane. 'Understand?'

'How much kerosene do you have in your store?' Mehra growls, his eyes narrowing to slits.

'About two kegs. I don't know exactly how many litres,' Bindal says. 'I fill up old beer or country liquor bottles to sell. Why?'

Mehra smiles.

'Veeru, use a roll of cheap linen and start cutting strips for wicks, about two feet in length. Ask Punit to help you. And move fast!'

47

'Sir, the ambulance should be here in about fifteen to twenty minutes,' Gulshan says, replacing the wireless handset in its holder.

'Why so long?' Satpal asks.

'Uh—the attendants were finishing their lunch,' Gulshan says with a shrug. Satpal snorts.

'I don't know what is taking Kultar this long to bring the driver and passengers here for a statement,' Satpal says, putting on his cap. 'I am going down to check.'

'Control Room is asking if we need any reinforcement…'

'For what?' Satpal asks over his shoulder. 'A silly road accident? We can handle this. We won't hear the end of it from the station head if we ask for more men, that motherfucker.'

Satpal walks towards the accident spot, pushing people out of his way. He breaks through the last cordon and stops over the injured Ali. Next to the boy, his wailing sister is surrounded by people supporting her, consoling her. Kultar is arguing with the driver.

'What's all this?' Satpal booms. 'Move back from the boy. Give space. What is happening, Kultar? Why didn't you bring these people for the preliminary statement?'

'Sir, the woman is refusing to come out,' Kultar complains. 'And this driver—Suraj Thakur—is not listening to me. They have already called some lawyer.'

'Sahib, please help my Ali, sahib,' Fatima runs to Satpal and falls at his feet, clutching his arms. 'These people tried to kill my brother.'

'Officer, this beggar is lying,' Suraj shouts, getting out of the car. 'That boy jumped right in front of our car. It is an accident. They-they just want to make money out of such situations.'

'Let go of me,' Satpal says, shaking away Fatima's grip on his arms. 'And mister, it is *our* job to find out who is lying. I can see you are on the wrong side of the road. Why are you not cooperating with my constable?'

'Sahib, this man saw Ali and still did not stop,' Fatima wails. 'These rich folks think they can do anything to us. Allah will take revenge on him.'

'I am not scared of your Allah, you filthy beggar,' Suraj shouts back. 'Another word and I will—'

'What will you do?' Fatima screams back. 'Will you drive your car over me too? Allah sees everything! He will curse your life and the lives of your whole family—you motherfucking infidel.'

She lunges at Suraj, scratching and clawing. Suraj pushes her away and slaps her in the face. Fatima staggers and falls, and an angry roar rises from the crowd.

48

'Shit!' Malaika groans. 'What the hell is Suraj doing?'

She unlocks her door and leaps out of the car. Priscilla looks at Lorna and immediately follows her boss.

'Officer, just look at that woman,' Malaika says, turning on Satpal, her nostrils flared and eyes wide with righteous fury. 'She—she just attacked my colleague in front of your eyes while you stand here doing nothing.'

'Madam, that boy your car hit is this woman's brother,' Satpal says. 'Your colleague has no right to hit her.'

'Oh yeah? And she can claw his eyes out?' Malaika hisses. 'Is this your idea of law and order? Who pays for your salary and uniform? People like *me* and *my colleague* here—*not* that beggar. And now you side with *her*? You stupid man!'

'Don't talk to a police officer in uniform in this manner,' Satpal warns. 'Or else—'

'Or else what?' Malaika snaps back. 'Just because I am a woman, you think you can threaten and abuse me? I will tell the media about how the police force treats women. And I will complain to your commissioner—I know him. Remember you are a bloody servant and *we* taxpayers are your masters!'

'How dare you, shameless woman!' Deepak shouts, stepping forward. 'Don't try to show off your contacts. We will show you who is the real master—*we*, the common people.'

'You cannot speak like that to a lady,' Priscilla protests, looking at Satpal. 'Sir, you have to keep this bunch of uncouth men away.'

Deepak screws up his face and pulls the corners of his eyes with his forefingers, making them slanting slits, and screams, 'Chinkie!'

'You sick bastard!' Priscilla spits. She ducks under Satpal's restraining arm and kicks Deepak between his legs. He groans and bends over in pain. Ramji steps forward and grabs Priscilla's collar to pull her away from Deepak. There is a loud ripping sound, as her shirt tears easily, exposing a flimsy, lacy bra.

49

'Oh, my God!' Thoi screams, pointing at the altercation outside. 'He just tore that woman's shirt in public! This is horrible! See, this is how they treat women from my region. I hate it—*I just hate it*!'

Angad cannot stay still any longer. He gets up and walks purposefully towards the exit. After a moment of hesitation, his friends follow him out, rushing past Titus and his friends looking at the scene unfolding outside with growing concern. Their expressions turn to worry as they see a black woman step out of the SUV and try to place herself between the crowd and the woman whose shirt had just been ripped.

50

'Shame on you!' Lorna hisses at Ramji, standing there with a dumbstruck expression, still clutching the torn fabric. 'You all are animals! Have you no respect for women in your country? Officer, why the hell are you not doing anything?' She takes off her scarf and drapes it over Priscilla's shoulder.

Satpal signals Kultar and the two move to herd the group back towards the PCR van. As the crowd realizes that the group is being moved away from the spot, they start shifting restlessly and begin to move in unison towards the police vehicle. Hari Shankar finds himself at the forefront of the crowd, being pushed forward unintentionally. Suraj jumps between his colleagues and the angry crowd, his arms stretched out protectively.

The crowd surges and Hari Shankar slams into Suraj, who shoves him back and punches him in the stomach. With a whimper of pain, Hari Shankar falls to his knees.

This is the last straw. The crowd raises a manic howl, and men and women alike charge at the retreating group, their hands raised, eyes burning with fury. At a command from Satpal, Kultar starts swinging his cane viciously, striking blindly.

Several hands claw at Lorna and she screams, as the crowd closes in on them.

51

The group of African students look on in horror.

'We must do something, Titus,' Faith begs with tears in her eyes. '*Now!*'

Idris leaps out of his chair and dashes to the door. Victor follows, swearing under his breath.

'Faith, Sharon—stay put,' Titus hisses, his eyes narrowed and fingers shaking a warning. 'We've got this.' Victor leads the way, followed by Idris and Titus, as they rush down the street towards the crowd. They spot Lorna near the car, being dragged away by some men. Idris races ahead, shoves and pushes his way into the crowd. A man charges at him with an angry shout. Idris jabs the heel of his palm under the man's jaw that slams shut on his tongue. Blood flows down the man's chin as he screams in pain.

Two men turn on Idris and try to pull him down to the street. Victor rams into them, his fists pounding whatever comes in the way while Titus rushes past towards Lorna. He hears a scream and halts in his tracks. 'Titus, help!'

Turning around, he sees Faith and Sharon being shoved by the mob. Behind him, he can hear Lorna cry out for help too. A few feet away, Victor and Idris are embattled with another group of men—probably construction workers—their faces masked in dried white paint. Titus casts his eyes about in desperation and spots Angad in the chaos. The young Sikh and his friends are struggling to slow down the horde pursuing the retreating policemen shepherding the passengers of the SUV away from the scene.

'Somebody please help me!' Titus hears Lorna's scream for help. The crowd has pushed Lorna back against the SUV and someone yanks the passenger door open. A stocky, short man slams her chest, and she falls backwards on the seat, her fuchsia skirt riding up her thighs.

52

'I suspect Satpal is going to take those people away from here,' Khalid says, shading his eyes with one hand. He is standing atop a small metal toolbox for a better view of the events unfolding down the street.

'If he manages to leave with them, we will not get anything more than insurance money for Ali,' Bashir says with a scowl. 'They will get some lawyer at the station and it will become difficult to negotiate for money.'

'We cannot allow that! We must hold them here till they pay a decent amount to us and Fatima,' Khalid says. 'It seems like the problem has escalated. Look! Kultar is caning the crowd ... and something else is happening near the car. I-I can't see clearly.'

'Take some boys and stop Satpal from driving away,' Bashir orders his boys. 'And ask all your friends to reach here immediately. We will need a crowd of ... our own people.'

54

'What the hell is Khalid up to?' Bindal asks, sipping from the bottle. His ill-fitting new kurta is stretched across his large belly and the pyjamas are riding too high above his plump ankles.

Mehra gulps from his bottle and squints against the harsh sun. Khalid and four young men are walking purposefully towards the parked police vehicle.

'I can see Satpal and his men escorting a group of women towards the PCR van—do you see?' Mehra observes.

'Ah—they are the people from the SUV that rammed into that Ali,' Bindal says, craning his neck. 'I recognize them. But … I think there are some other people in the group—understand?'

'I don't trust Khalid,' Mehra says. 'He must be on some crooked mission from Bashir. Have you called our friends, Veeru?'

'They should be on their way,' Veeru replies. 'I asked them to … uh … come prepared, as you asked.'

'Excellent, excellent,' Mehra nods. 'Take Punit and try to find out what Khalid and his men are planning. Oh—and, also, find out what all that screaming and shouting is about. Who is coordinating today?'

'Uh, I thought you wanted some action today,' Veeru says, scratching his stubble. 'So … I asked Monty to …'

'Hmm, good,' Mehra nods approvingly. 'Call him and tell him not to bring the men here for now. I don't want to alert Bashir. Ask them to mingle with that crowd and stay ready for action when I say. And get the kerosene bombs ready.'

55

'Karl, Karl!' Angad calls out to his friend. 'Keep the group together and follow the policemen. I have to help that lady back there.'

'Don't be stupid, Angad,' Thoi shouts over her shoulder. 'We have to stick together!'

'There are many of us, Thoi,' Angad shouts back, pushing away a couple of people to move ahead. 'That woman is alone, crying for help. We can't just walk away. Go with Karl and the others—I'll come back with that woman.'

'No, wait!' Thoi pleads, but Angad has already disappeared into the melee.

'Thoi, we need to keep moving,' Karl says, firmly pushing her ahead. 'He will be fine. He can take care of himself.'

56

Suraj also hears Lorna's cry and looks back. He can't see her but thinks she is somewhere near their car.

'Keep moving,' Satpal hisses. 'We have to get away from the crowd and into the police vehicle. Don't stop moving till we reach the safety of the van.'

'Suraj, Suraj!' Malaika wails. 'That's Lorna. She's stuck back there. We need to get her.'

'What can I do?' Suraj snaps back, shoving people away. 'You heard the policeman. Keep moving.'

'But … but Lorna is all alone,' Priscilla whimpers. 'She is not safe.'

'Neither are *we*, Pris,' Suraj retorts. 'Once we get you to the police car, I will ask these policemen to get her. For now, just keep moving. I think that Sikh fellow is trying to help Lorna. Keep moving.'

Suddenly, Suraj steps into a pothole, trips and falls with a painful thud. The crowd shuffle and stomp around him, raising dust. He covers himself with his arms, trying to save himself from the relentless onslaught of shins and heels.

57

'Wait near the van for Satpal and others,' Khalid tells the four boys following him. 'Don't let them get away. Bashir Bhai needs to talk to them. I will go and check on Fatima and Ali in some time.'

'Why bother about those beggars, Khalid Bhai?' one of the boys asks.

'Fatima has two little kids with her,' Khalid says, starting to walk away. 'They can rest in the garage.'

'Why?' the boy asks again.

Khalid turns to look at the boy. The boy instantly lowers his eyes.

'I have known Fatima for a long time. She is one of our own. So are her kids and her brother. Fatima delivered both her kids in my garage,' he paces out each word. 'That's why I care. I can't abandon them to this crazy mob.' Turning on his heels, Khalid marches off into the thick of the crowd.

58

Hari Shankar manages to stand up. He clutches his stomach and winces with pain. He sees that one of the passengers is surrounded by an angry mob, but the rest of her companions are missing. He takes a hesitant step towards the big, black SUV, but stops as he feels a tug on his hand. He looks down to see Nafisa holding on to him, fearfully.

A woman's scream pulls his attention back to the car. The mob, led by a short, stocky man, jeers loudly. Then the rest of the crowd stops a short distance away, growing quieter, watching with unholy expectation as the stocky man moves into the car. Hari Shankar cannot see exactly what is happening, but he has lived too long on the streets not to know the mindless cruelty of mobs. He sends a silent prayer to his gods for the woman.

The women start separating from the angry mob and move away to protect themselves. They huddle in small groups along the park fence and under trees. They watch mutely as the men transform from beaten, deprived dregs to a restless, growling pack of predators that will destroy or self-destruct. The women watch in fascination. They watch in satisfaction. They watch in fear.

Hari Shankar spots Fatima, who is standing with her back against a tree, hugging her boy. There is little he can do to help. He pushes his cart and blocks the scared girl and her children from the mob.

59

Satpal walks backwards behind Kultar, who is swinging his cane frantically to stop the mob. But the mob is relentless and determined. One man falls down and another takes his place. Their faces are blank and eyes empty of emotions. There is no rage, no fury—just determination. As they close in, Kultar feels his breath becoming laboured. With each swing, he seems to now miss the mark.

Cursing under his breath, Satpal draws his service pistol and clicks the safety off. Pushing Malaika and her colleague behind him, he raises his arm and fires. The sharp, loud bang rings out over the noise. A surprised Kultar stumbles. But the crowd continues to close in. Satpal curses loudly, sidesteps and lowers his weapon at the men. He hesitates a moment, then fires.

A man screams and falls to the ground, bleeding from his shin. The mob slows down, wavers and finally grinds to a halt. Satpal's lips stretch in a thin smile, and he steps past Kultar to stand in the empty strip of street between them and the crowd.

'No one will move!' he shouts. 'Do not follow us. Or else …' He fires another warning shot in the air.

60

The stone is disc-shaped and smooth. It is the same stone from under which Ali, just a while ago, had retrieved a leaf to plug the hole in his shoe. Around it, feet shuffle, trip and trample on the dusty ground. A leathery hand turns it, picks it up to weigh it in the palm. The stone fits well in the hard hollow of the palm that curls around it in a fist. The arm arcs back and hurls the stone.

With a slow, elliptical trajectory the stone flies through rebelling dust above heads seething with anger and dips on its random path of destruction. Its fall is inevitable and so is the end of reason it will mark and the carnage it will unleash.

It smashes into the glass window of the pub, shattering it with a loud crash.

PART TWO
Enflamed

61

A stone smashes against the windscreen, leaving behind a jagged web of cracks and fissures on it.

Lorna stops her frantic thrashing and her eyes lock into those of the man standing between her legs. *Why*, she wants to scream, *what have I done to you?* Beyond the man's shoulder, she can see a sea of faces—impassive, unmoved. Her throat is dry. She can hear the pounding of her heart. She opens her mouth to beg for help, but finds her voice reduced to a meaningless, broken screech. She tries to push her skirt down her thighs, but the man grabs her wrists and stops her. Then, he moves closer and pushes her knees apart.

His hands feel rough on her thighs, the nails digging into her flesh. They furrow across her skin, leaving shameful ruts. Lorna's mind orders her legs to kick and lash out, but her limbs do not respond. The roving hands end their journey where her legs meet. A strange hand hooks into the flimsy fabric and yanks. Moments later, sounds, colours, smells ... everything swoops in from everywhere and squashes her soul.

It ends as abruptly as it had started. Then it starts again And again, till everything ceases to exist.

62

Angad pushes against the wall of inert bodies with all his strength but cannot breach it. He can feel the electric thrill of the wall of people standing between him and the SUV. Above their heads, he sees the roof of the vehicle sway to an unholy rhythm.

'Let me through,' he raises his voice, pressing with his shoulders. 'I am an army officer.'

Four white-coated faces with red-rimmed eyes turn upon him. He stops pushing.

'There ...' he says, panting. 'There is a woman near the car. She needs help. Please ... let me pass.'

The faces stare at him—eyes unblinking and lips set tight.

'Army?' Angad says with some hope. 'Officer? Understand?'

Four pairs of eyes scrutinize him.

'Let me through, my friend,' Angad tries again. 'That woman is in danger. Stand back! I am an army officer.'

The four men share a look and look back at him. They move in on Angad together, forcing him to take a step back from the wall of people. Angad puts up his hands and takes a fighting stance. The four men instantly fan out in a rough arc. Angad moves like a flash, leading with a left jab aimed at the squat man directly in front of him. But the man ducks away and swiftly punches Angad's stomach, knocking the wind out of him. As Angad gasps for breath, another man slams a knee into his chest and drives a vicious elbow into the nape of his neck. The pain is blinding and Angad drops to his knees, crouching and clutching his stomach.

He expects more blows but several moments pass and nothing happens. When he looks up, the four assailants have disappeared. Before him is a stockade of human flesh and bones.

63

Fatima clutches her child to her breast as her daughter clings to the hem of her grimy kameez. She spots Ali, still lying on the street—uncared for and unattended. Beyond him, the black SUV has been surrounded by the angry mob. Its frame shakes violently for a few moments, then becomes still. But only briefly—then it starts rocking again. Her eyes well up with tears.

Hari Shankar lowers his gaze when Fatima points a trembling finger at the SUV. She pulls her daughter closer and turns to the huddle of women with grim faces, gazing at the shaking car. Some scowl at Fatima as she whimpers and raises a hand to the sky. Others hang their heads and look away.

Fatima shakes her head in disbelief and puts her baby down on the pavement, shushing him with gentle sounds. She pats his back and places him near her five-year-old daughter.

'Take care of your little brother, Nafisa,' she says, caressing her daughter's head.

The girl nods and hugs Murad. Fatima smiles and walks over to Ali. She places a finger under his nose and checks for breath. Then she puts her palms on Ali's chest and feels for a heartbeat. She looks up at Hari Shankar with a quivering smile. He nods back several times with a grin of relief and reassurance.

His expression changes to shock as Fatima gets up and starts walking towards the SUV.

'No, Fatima!' Hari Shankar screams. 'Don't …'

64

'Here, take my hand,' a voice booms from above as a big, strong hand reaches out to Angad. 'Get up, man. We need to get away from here quickly.'

Angad shakes his head to clear his vision, grabs the hand and stands up. The two African women from the group are standing behind Titus, looking anxious.

'Di-did you see any of my friends?' Angad asks.

'N-no! I was too busy trying to keep these ladies out of trouble. Sorry,' Titus says apologetically. 'But have you seen my brothers? They were right behind you and your friends.'

'Yeah, they were behind me,' Angad says. 'I-I was trying to make my way to the SUV … a bunch of people attacked a lady from the car. She was alone. I—'

'I know,' Titus nods. 'My friends and I were trying to reach her too.'

'It's not safe here, for women,' Angad says. 'Listen, the policemen have escorted my friends to the police van. No one will dare attack a police vehicle. Maybe we should first take these ladies to the police and then come back to find your friends.'

'Sounds right, my friend,' Titus says. 'Let's go.'

65

Fatima tries to squeeze through the men around the car.

'Let me through,' she says, trying to push them away. 'In the name of Allah! Leave that woman alone!'

The man turns around with a sneer. Fatima bangs a puny fist against his shoulder in anger. The man grunts and shoves her away. Fatima staggers but lunges back, pummelling his back with both her fists.

The man turns around and looks at her. His face is darkened with hate and his eyes are enflamed. He takes in her delicate, oval face with full lips and her young and curvaceous body. With a slow smile, he grabs her wrists and pulls her into the vortex of the crowd.

Fatima allows herself to be dragged. Her eyes dart in every direction, looking for the black woman. The man holds both her wrists in one big hand and parts the crowd blocking their way.

They emerge into a small, empty circle near the SUV. Fatima gasps as she spots a woman's legs dangling lifelessly from the back seat of the vehicle. A man is buttoning up his frayed trousers as he walks away from the car.

Fatima panics and tries to break free but the man's grip is strong. He pulls her towards the vehicle and men make way for him.

'Please ... please let me go,' Fatima wails. 'I have two small children waiting for me ... please ...'

The man continues to drag her till they reach the car. He puts his big hands on her slim shoulders and pushes her against the bonnet.

'Please, I-I just wanted to help,' she whimpers.

The man turns her back towards the still vehicle and slams her frail body against the bonnet.

66

Victor and Idris are blocked by a ring of a dozen men.

One man lunges at Victor, who sidesteps and delivers a nasty left hook, bringing his attacker down. He hops over the prostrate man and jabs at the next person in his path. The crowd moves back a little, leaving a rough circle around the two friends. Victor looks around but doesn't see Titus. Neither can he locate Faith or Sharon. He sighs with relief and beckons Idris to move closer. The crowd is too dense for them to penetrate, so they start making their way around the crowd. A few youngsters try to stop them, but Victor makes short work of them. His knuckles are raw and bleeding by now, but he doesn't care. Idris covers the back and flank. He is a master with his broad leather belt that he swings in lethal arcs to keep the crowd at bay.

Emerging from the crowd, Victor finds himself near an ice cream cart. The accident victim, a boy, is lying on the street in a pool of blood. An old man is standing close by with a little girl by his side, clutching the hand of an even younger boy. Near them, there is a bunch of women—watching with hostile eyes.

What is wrong with everyone? Are they going mad? Who is the kid on the ground? Why isn't anyone helping him?

'Id—this boy seems to be alive—his chest is moving,' Victor says, breathing heavily. 'Let's try to get him away from crazy mob.'

Idris nods and they move towards Ali's prone body. The women let out a loud wail. Taken aback, Victor and Idris stop. Idris raises his hands in a reconciliatory gesture. A woman starts howling. Then another one. The two friends stand, perplexed, as many more voices join in the eerie ululation.

'We are trying to help the boy,' Idris says out loud. 'We don't mean any harm ... please.'

The women only wail louder. One of them steps forward and stands between Ali and the two African boys. Some of the men in the outermost circle facing the SUV turn around and watch with interest.

'Look—calm down,' Victor says in an even voice, his palms extended towards the woman. He steps forward and gently holds her shoulders, trying to soothe her.

A shrill caterwaul rises from the gang of women. Victor looks up in surprise and lets go of the woman's shoulder. He has no time to evade the piece of broken brick that hits him in the head and cracks his temporal bone. He slumps to the ground even as Idris tries to shield him with his own body. The hail of bricks and stones that follows is accurate and cruel. At first, there are only a few. But as the two African boys go down, the intensity of brickbats increases. Soon, it is a veritable barrage. Some of the women join the fray, picking up pebbles to pelt Victor and Idris.

It goes on till their bodies are still and their heads reduced to pulp.

67

'Looks like people are pelting stones, understand?' Bindal says, craning his neck.

Mehra follows his friend's gaze. Indeed, there is more commotion near the SUV. He can see stones and bricks fly. They seem to be targeting someone near the spot where the ice cream cart is parked.

'Excellent!' Mehra says, taking another swig. 'That arrogant sub-inspector deserves it. This is a golden opportunity for us.'

'How, bhai fa'ab?' Sonu asks with a reverential look.

Mehra ignores him and takes out his cell phone.

'Monty? How are you, my son?' Mehra asks. 'Excellent, excellent. I hope Veeru delivered my instructions, yes? Excellent. Oh, are your men already in the crowd? Excellent! Now listen carefully—I can see Khalid and some of his boys are about to create trouble and start a fight here. They want an excuse to attack us. Now listen carefully …'

Bindal and the others huddle closer to Mehra.

'… the situation is tense now,' Mehra says. 'The sub-inspector is shooting at the crowd. This will escalate into a bigger chaos. I know Bashir is planning to take advantage of the situation. I want to take them by surprise. The moment you see Khalid and his men engage the police, I want your men to start pelting stones at the PCR. Tell them to aim well and try to get Khalid—he is Bashir's right-hand man. I want him out of the way before anything starts. Everyone will blame it on the crowd. Got it? Excellent, excellent.'

'What a fantaftic plan, bhai fa'ab!' Sonu exclaims with admiration. 'With Khalid and his boyf injured, Bafhir won't have anyone to execute his evil planf.'

Bindal grins and thumps Mehra on the shoulder. They clink their bottles in a toast.

68

'I wonder what is making those two so happy?' Junaid asks Bashir. 'Did they not hear the gunshots?'

The old man caresses his beard and looks at Mehra and Bindal raising a toast. He follows their gaze to Khalid and his men talking to the PCR driver, Gulshan. There is a throng of nearly 500 people clogging the street now, angry and vengeful.

He surveys the hopelessly jammed street with narrowed eyes, evaluating the situation. Vehicles had tried to wiggle past others or turn around. Some ended up ramming into each other and, eventually, blocking the narrow street at both ends. Several people are trapped inside their cars as there is no space for opening their doors, which are blocked by other cars. Those who could have run away.

The inner circle of the crowd is shouting and pelting stones at someone.

'I don't like it, Junaid,' Bashir says finally. 'At first, they were pelting that SUV with stones—I can understand that. But that has stopped now. Satpal must have fired warning shots. I just can't understand who is throwing brickbats now and at whom. It seems very random.'

'Crowds get crazy, Khan Chacha,' Junaid shrugs. 'I saw a riot once. Many people died. Houses were robbed and burned down. A cinema hall was vandalized. No one quite found out who started it.'

'Oh, the communal riots are different,' Bashir says, his eyes clouding up. 'Often, there is a hidden agenda. But this? Unless …' He turns to look at Mehra and Bindal again. Mehra was once again on the phone.

'I smell something,' Bashir tells Junaid. 'Call up our other people and ask them to get here immediately. I think Mehra is trying to pull a trick on us.'

69

In the push and pull of the crowd, Bonium leads Thoi out of the chaos, but they find themselves cut off from the rest of the group. He yells out to Satpal who is now in rapid retreat, herding the remaining group.

Seeing their plight, Satpal lets off another shot. It hits a man in his shoulder. People scream and run helter-skelter, knocking each other down, leaping over fallen bodies and cars, screaming in rage and panic. There is no way Satpal can reach Thoi and Bonium now.

'I will put them in the PCR and come back for you,' Satpal shouts above the roar of the crowd. 'Don't do anything stupid. Find a safe corner and don't attract attention. Merge with the crowd. I'll be back soon.'

Thoi looks at Bonium with panicked eyes. The boy is sweating profusely and his face is flushed. His breath comes out in short gasps with a dry, wheezing noise.

'Are you getting an asthma attack, Boni?' she asks, putting an arm around him. Bonium nods weakly.

'Angad is somewhere near the SUV,' Thoi says. 'Let's make our way back to him. It's not safe here.'

She leads the way through the crowd and Bonium follows her, struggling to breathe. Thoi tries to spot the car over the crowd.

Thoi also keeps her eyes peeled for Angad's scarlet turban, but it is nowhere in sight. She spots the black, shiny roof of the SUV above the heads of men swarming around her and her face lights up.

'It's them! That Chinkie girl was in the car. Grab them!'

The crowd bears down on Thoi and Bonium, and she starts pushing and screaming.

'W-we were not in that car!' Thoi yells.

Bonium pushes away another man trying to stop them. The man screams in rage and slaps Bonium's face. The boy cries out in pain and Thoi slaps the man back in reflex.

'You bastard, stay back,' she cries.

Several hands reach out and drag Bonium down to the gravelly street. Someone kicks him in the belly and the boy doubles up in pain. Another shoe grinds on Bonium's upturned palm and stamps on it. Bonium's scream turns into a shrill, choking wheeze as his lips turn blue and his eyes bulge out.

'Let him be, you animals!' Thoi screams. 'He is just a school kid. Stop!'

She hurls herself at the men kicking and punching Bonium but is pulled short by the man she had slapped. He wraps an arm around her tiny waist and drags her back as she continues to thrash. But the man has far more strength.

'Hit him!' a voice exhorts. 'These Chinkies are ruining our town—bloody druggies and sluts.'

'Look at the clothes she is wearing,' another voice shrieks. 'The bitch.'

'They don't belong here,' a third voice says.

'Make the pig bleed!'

'Strip her!'

Everyone who gets a chance kicks Bonium, who is now bleeding profusely from his nose and mouth. Thoi sobs and begs for mercy with palms pressed together.

Bonium splutters out bubbles of blood. A few more kicks land on his body, which jerks once or twice, then lies absolutely still.

Thoi freezes as she looks at his still body. She finds no voice as she is hauled away from the scene. She staggers behind the man dragging her, her confused eyes flitting from face to face. She says nothing as hands reach out and touch her—here, there, everywhere. She stands in a daze when they break out of the crowd into an empty semi-circle around the SUV. She gazes with befuddlement as a loud cheer rises around her. She doesn't even protest when the man throws her against the hot bonnet of the SUV and lifts the hem of her dress.

70

'Yes, yes, I said Code Green,' Gulshan yells into the radio handset. 'Need immediate reinforcement. SI Satpal has fired four rounds. Over.'

'Stay there at the location,' the static voice on the receiver crackles. 'We are sending in reinforcements. Over-and-out.'

'Motherfucker! *Stay there?* Where the hell do you think we can move?' Gulshan spits at the mouthpiece and slams it back in its mount. He starts rummaging for something under his seat.

'What is going on, uncle?' Khalid says, leaning on the window. 'You look scared. Is everything fine?'

Gulshan looks up at Khalid's smiling face and sighs. Shaking his head, he gets back to his quest. With a grunt, he pulls out a piece of lead pipe about two feet long. He yanks the door lever and pushes against Khalid to open the door.

'Oh-ho, uncle,' Khalid says, chuckling and moving away. 'You are getting stronger with age. What's that nasty weapon for?'

'What?' Gulshan demands, his face flushed. 'Are you blind, smartass? Can't you see or hear that madness on the street?'

Khalid turns to his men and smiles. They grin back.

'Do you see anything, boys?' he asks. 'Hear anything?'

'We see an old man with a stiff rod in his hand,' Aslam quips, snorting.

'And we hear his loud farts,' another youngster adds.

'See? Uncle? Nothing unusual going on,' Khalid says. 'It's just a regular hot afternoon. A regular accident. A regular reaction from the people around. Why are you so worried?'

'Look, you prick—there's nothing regular about this,' Gulshan says, slamming the PCR's door behind him. 'I have seen such things for more years than you have lived. The crowd is going mad.'

'Mad?' Khalid says, rounding his eyes and looking around. It draws appropriate sniggers from his men. 'It's the heat, uncle. They are just blowing off some steam. And your boss is shooting some bullets—that's all. Take it easy.'

'What the hell do you want?' Gulshan asks, craning his neck to follow the movement of Satpal's group through the crowd.

'I want peace on earth,' Khalid says with an expansive flourish of his arms, drawing more derisive laughter from his adoring men. 'I want equality, freedom, harmony, love, prosperity ... Are you selling?'

The men burst out laughing.

'Asshole!'

'Why are you getting angry, uncle?' Khalid asks, blocking Gulshan's view. 'Give me the car's key.'

'Why?'

'So that you don't drive off with those snooty, rich bastards who rammed into my little brother Ali. They have to pay up.'

'Do you think anyone will be able to drive off?' Gulshan asks, his eyes widening in disbelief. He waves at the scores of cars logjammed in the street. Not one vehicle can move an inch. 'Don't you see that?' He jabs at the surging crowd with a stubby finger.

Khalid turns to look at the crowd again and exclaims with surprise.

'Wow, your boss is the real hero today, uncle,' he says. Everyone turns to the scene unfolding behind them.

Satpal has his pistol ready in a classic two-handed grip. He walks backwards, legs planted in a high, horse-riding stance and feet sliding across the street, feeling for any obstruction in his path. He moves the barrel in a wide arc, keeping the oncoming horde at bay. Behind him, constables Kultar and Amit guide the group towards the PCR. They have almost extricated themselves from the thickest part of the crowd and are within a few feet of the PCR now.

'I have many bullets still left,' Satpal roars. 'Do not follow us beyond this point. Do not take the law into your hands. This is my last warning. Next time, I will shoot to kill.'

Khalid whistles softly and leans his elbow on the bonnet. Gulshan gives him a tired look and rushes forward towards Satpal's group with the lead pipe swinging in his hand.

The crowd stops moving. The frontline halts and people pile up against it, forming an impenetrable human wall.

Seeing the opportunity, Satpal gestures to the others to run for the PCR. He stands still, covering their backs—slowly swivelling his pistol.

Gulshan greets the group and takes them to the PCR. He opens the tailgate of the van and ushers Malaika, Priscilla and

Uma into the back seats. The bench-like seats in the rear can squeeze in eight passengers.

Karl, Partho and Raunak choose to stay out and huddle at the rear of the PCR, waiting for Satpal. Soon, Satpal joins them and receives words of thanks and pats from everyone.

71

Titus pushes through the crowd and the rest follow him in a file, with Angad at the tail end. They are deep inside the belly of the pulsating crowd.

Angad stems a fresh trickle of blood from his nose with his handkerchief. Men and women jostle around him in a catatonic frenzy—eyes glazed, faces contorted in a mix of fear, exhilaration and rage. He feels a hand on his shoulder and turns to find a man in his thirties—with his face bruised and swollen up, his clothes in tatters and barely able to stand.

'Help—please!' Suraj gasps. 'I don't know where my colleagues are. We were in the SUV together ...'

'Oh—okay,' Angad says. 'The other two ladies are with the police, I think ...'

A surge of men barges in between Angad and Suraj.

'Please!'

'I'm sorry,' Angad shouts over his shoulder. 'We have two other women with us. We have to get them to safety first. Just wait here ... I'll be back for you very soon. Stay put by that lamp-post, I will find you!'

In a moment, Angad loses sight of Suraj. He sees Titus halt against a thick cluster of men and women and presses on towards Titus and the two women stuck against a thick cluster of bodies.

As soon as he reaches them, they hear a gunshot, followed by another.

'Jesus!' Titus says, turning to Angad. 'What's that?'

'Sounds like a standard issue Glock 17 to me,' Angad says. 'Thankfully, it is a police weapon. I think that cop has opened fire. Good for him!'

'Oh God, we're stuck,' Sharon sobs. 'Oh please, please, please, I am so scared.'

'Hey, calm down,' Titus barks. 'Get a grip, girl. We just have to find a way to get to the cops and the others. We'll be safe.'

'How do we get through?' Faith asks, hugging Sharon.

'Crawl,' Angad says. 'Get down on your fours and crawl.'

'What?' Titus is incredulous.

'Trust me, it works,' Angad says, getting down on his knees. 'They taught this in our mob control classes. People don't know how to react if you crawl between their legs—they wouldn't think of you as a threat. They will resist us if we try to push through.'

He starts crawling through the undergrowth of legs, butting with his head and shoulders. Most people just shift their legs and let him pass. Some look down, then look away—craning their necks to see what is happening around them. Someone has started building up an angry chant.

'Policemen, hai, hai! Death to policemen!' the crowd thunders. 'Every enemy of this town—will be truly broken down!'

'Holy crap—it really works!' Titus grins and gets down on his knees. 'Come on, girls, our soldier friend is bloody right.'

In a couple of minutes, they break the barrier of the crowd and reach the vacant space that had been demarcated by Satpal just moments ago with a bullet shot at the sky.

72

Men work at a frenzied pace with dark frowns and bated breath in the basement of Bindal's shop. They talk in whispers as they fill up empty beer bottles with kerosene from two large aluminium tanks. Some stuff the wicks in the bottles. Others relay them upstairs to the back of the shop where Vikas and Punit help them stack the bottles on racks that have been emptied of hardware boxes.

'Excellent, excellent,' Mehra says, walking into Bindal's shop. 'How many bottles do we have now?'

Bindal turns to Punit and raises his eyebrows, swigging from his bottle of Sprite.

'Uh, we have about thirty already filled up and stacked here,' Punit says. 'I think another twenty are getting ready in the basement.'

'Excellent, excellent,' Mehra pats Bindal's round belly. 'This will be enough for anything that Bashir tries.'

'I'm here,' a big voice booms from the shop entrance. Everyone turns to look at the giant blocking the door.

'Oh-ho, Monty, my good boy,' Mehra smiles and walks across to embrace the young man with bulbous shoulders and thick arms. He has a broad, sloping forehead, crowned with a shock of curly hair. When he smiles, he flashes a gold-covered incisor.

'Our men are ready, Mehra Uncle,' Monty says, breaking the hug. 'Thirty-four. They are armed with stones, rods ... some have knives. Two have country-made pistols. Bottles ready?'

'Indeed, indeed,' Bindal preens. 'But how will you distribute them ... people ... police ... understand?'

Monty scowls at the question. 'My problem,' he says. 'Not yours.'

'We are doing this because—'

'—not interested,' Monty cuts Bindal short. 'I like doing this. The reason is not important.'

'Okay, okay, go and wait inside Bindal's shop and keep some sturdy lads with you,' Mehra says. 'On my command, get your boys to ignite the kerosene bombs and target Khalid's garage and his men surrounding the PCR. Make sure you take Gidwani with you—he has a pistol.'

Monty grunts and nods his head. He strides past Bindal, bumping him aside, followed by two of his own goons.

73

Murad tugs at his sister's frock and sniffles. Nafisa pulls him closer, and he stands peering out from behind her.

'Where is Ammi?' Nafisa asks.

'She—she has gone to sell some flowers,' Hari Shankar says.

'But her basket is lying here,' Nafisa says, pointing at Fatima's basket of flowers.

'Ammi?' her little brother asks.

'She will be back soon,' Ramji says. 'Why don't you have an ice cream? Hari Shankar?'

Hari Shankar opens the lid of the freezer and takes out a bundle of ice cream sticks.

'Which one do you want?'

'I don't want any,' Nafisa says. 'I want Ammi.'

'Come on, have one,' Deepak cajoles. 'Your Ammi is just down the road—beyond that big black car.'

'Then take me to her.'

'Uh—she is busy,' Hari Shankar says. 'She will be angry if I take you and disturb her work.'

'I can walk that far,' Nafisa says, grabbing her brother's hand.

'No!' Hari Shankar and Ramji shout at the same time. They exchange glances.

Inside Burn

'I want to.'

'You can't go now.'

'Why? Ammi won't scold me.'

'N-no, but she will scold me for letting you go alone,' Hari Shankar, says looking at his friends for help.

'You are older,' Nafisa counters. 'She can't scold you.'

'Have an ice cream.'

'I don't want to.'

'Ammi?' Murad whimpers.

'Does your doll want ice cream?' Ramji asks.

'Dolls don't eat real food,' Nafisa says with a frown. 'I want to go to Ammi.'

'Here, give me your doll and let's see if she will eat,' Hari Shankar reaches out a hand.

'Her mouth doesn't work,' Nafisa says, refusing to part with her doll. 'Her stomach only has air. Ammi says it would have been good if Murad and I were like this doll. Then she wouldn't have to work so hard to feed us.'

The men lower their eyes to the ground.

'You don't have children,' Nafisa observes after a moment of deep thought. 'Why do you sell ice cream all day?'

'Because I too have to earn to eat something,' Hari Shankar says with a smile. 'It is not just about feeding children.'

'What if you don't eat?'

'I will die.'

'Ammi says if she didn't have children she would want to die,' Nafisa says. 'You don't have children. Why don't you want to die?'

'I do have children, but they are not here,' Hari Shankar says. 'They live very far away—in my village.'

'You don't want them to live with you?' Nafisa is curious. 'Ammi says she cannot live away from us because she loves us very much. She loves Murad even more than she loves me. You don't love your children?'

'Of course, I love them a lot, Nafisa.'

'Then why don't you want them here?' Nafisa counters. 'I love Ammi. I want to go to her.'

'She will be back very soon,' Deepak says. 'Have patience.'

Nafisa stares at Deepak for a long time, till he looks away. Murad puts a thumb in his mouth and Nafisa pulls it out. The boy sticks his thumb back in again.

'You really love your children like Ammi loves us?' Nafisa asks Hari Shankar.

'Absolutely.'

'Then do you want them to die?'

'What? Why would I want them dead?'

'Ammi says she loves us so much that sometimes she wants us to die.'

74

'Things don't look good, Khan Chacha,' Junaid says, cleaning the flimsy barrel of his country-made pistol, watching the crowd.

'Put that away,' Bashir snaps. 'Are our men ready?'

'I got calls confirming that,' Junaid says. 'We are ready.'

Bashir glares at the pistol and Junaid holds his gaze for a long time before sticking it in his belt. He pulls his shirt over the bulge.

'I think he has men in the crowd too. They may interfere with Khalid. We should just—'

'Didn't you hear the gunshots?' Bashir asks, helping himself to a cardamom from his silver box. He doesn't offer any to Junaid. 'We do nothing unless absolutely necessary.'

'So, if Mehra's men beat up Khalid, that is fine?'

'That won't happen,' Bashir grunts. 'Mehra isn't so foolish as to send men up to the PCR and start a fight. But I think they might use a group of men who will heckle the police and demand the SUV people be taken away to the lock-up. If that happens...'

'We target those hecklers and stone them?' Junaid asks with a crooked smile.

'Yes, create more panic and provoke a stampede around the police car,' Bashir nods. 'Let the crowd do our job for us. The stampede will block the route and Satpal will be distracted. And…'

'And?' Junaid asks, narrowing his eyes.

'We can use the moment to target Mehra, Bindal and their shops.'

'Now that sounds like a plan,' Junaid bobs his head with satisfaction. 'I saw Monty just come out of Mehra's shop with a couple of his boys.'

'Who?' Bashir looks up.

'His dad has a real estate agency in the south wing of this market. He loves to play rough.'

'And you don't?' Bashir asks.

'That's why I like your plan,' Junaid grins. 'I have some old issues to sort out with Monty.'

'Today is not about your grudges, Junaid,' Bashir remonstrates. 'It is about defending our faith.'

'It's always about my grudges, Khan Chacha,' Junaid says, patting the gun at his waist. 'I don't really care about any faith.'

75

Uma squeals with joy as she spots Angad crawl out of the crowd with the others.

'Our soldier is back,' Partho grins.

They dash to the PCR, accompanied by Gulshan and Kultar, and rush the small group back to the safety of the van. Gulshan barks a command and Amit drags up a stack of Nadar barriers that are lined up along the pavement. He places them in a zigzag formation across the street and slips the interconnecting hooks to form a makeshift barricade. Kultar runs his cane across the metal bars of the barrier making a loud, rattling noise. He glares at the faces in the front line of the truculent crowd till the slogans subside a little.

Satpal looks on with a sour expression at the newcomers. He takes off his sunglass and polishes them with great diligence.

'Welcome to the shelter,' he says, blowing on the glasses and rubbing them with his handkerchief.

Angad's friends hug him in turn while Titus and his companions hover in the background. Angad peers inside the PCR and finds just two women looking back at him.

'Wh-where is Thoi?' he asks. 'And Bonium?'

The friends search each other's eyes.

'Are they not here?' Angad asks, looking up and down the street.

'We ... we were in the thick of that crowd,' Karl says. 'The sub-inspector ...'

'Satpal,' he drawls, clarifying his own name. 'Sub-Inspector Satpal Choudhary.'

'Yes ... he and the other policeman ...' Karl continues.

'Kultar Sirohi,' Satpal adds with a helpful smile, donning his sunglasses.

'He ... they escorted us all out of that madness to safety,' Raunak blurts out.

'Not from enemy bullets, but from a crazy mob of *citizens*,' Satpal says, relishing every word. 'Not with tanks and heavy artillery. But with a stick and pistol. Defending *citizens* from dangerous *citizens*. Isn't that defending the nation too? Or do you think that protecting *citizens* and defending the nation are two different things?'

Satpal looks Angad in the eye.

'The thing is ...' Uma intervenes. 'We lost Thoi and Bonium in the crowd. We have to get them out. The inspector—uh—sub-inspector said he will go back for them.'

Angad looks at Satpal and nods. After a long pause, Satpal nods back.

'Look, I have two friends stuck in that mob,' Titus says. 'They need help too.'

'From me?' Satpal says, examining his Glock. 'Or from your embassy?'

'I am going back in,' Titus says. 'Faith, Sharon—wait for me here.'

'Titus! You can't—' Faith starts to protest.

'What do you suggest?' Titus turns to her. 'We stand here doing nothing?'

'We have to find Lorna and Suraj,' Malaika says from inside the PCR. 'They are in danger.'

'Suraj?' Angad asks. 'Was he with you in your SUV?'

'Yes, and Lorna,' Priscilla offers. 'She is French-American ... uh ... Afric—she's black.'

'I have seen the direction in which the crowd has pushed her,' Angad says. 'I will go back in and get them all out.'

'I will come with you,' Titus says.

'You can't go back,' Satpal says, shoving his pistol back in its holster. 'It's not safe.'

'So, who will go back for them?' Titus asks. 'You?'

'We cannot leave so many ladies unprotected here,' Angad points out. 'The sub-inspector has to stay back.'

'You trust me to protect them?' Satpal's eyes drill into Angad's.

'Yes,' Angad responds after a small pause. 'I understand what you said back there in the pub. You were right—I say.'

Satpal looks at Angad with a quizzical expression on his face. He opens his mouth to say something but decides against it.

'No one goes anywhere until—' Satpal's sentence is cut short by a call on his phone. He looks at the caller's name and takes the call, standing at attention.

'Sir!' he barks. 'Yes sir, I had to open fire—sir, I have two men with me ... no, sir ... yes, sir.'

Satpal walks away, beckoning to Kultar to follow.

'I guess he has to answer to his masters,' Titus says. 'And therefore, my friend ...?'

'Angad.'

'That leaves you and me to get the others back here.'

'You can't go,' Gulshan says, gripping his lead pipe. 'Wait till the sub-inspector returns. I won't let you go before that.'

76

Kultar waves his cane at Khalid and his men, and gestures at them to stay clear of Satpal's path as he walks away from the PCR. Khalid holds Kultar's gaze, refusing to budge.

Satpal continues talking on the phone in a hushed tone without breaking his stride and puts a hand on the butt of his pistol, looking at Khalid with a raised eyebrow. Khalid begins to say something, but Satpal holds up a hand to silence him and continues his slow, measured pace forward. Khalid holds his place. He sees Satpal's eyes narrow as he pulls the Glock halfway out of the holster.

Aslam tugs at Khalid's arm and whispers in his ear. Behind the PCR, the crowd is beginning to get restless again. The slogans of protest increase in volume and intensity. The frontline of the mob heaves and sways like waves in the ocean. But they maintain a few feet of distance from the barricade.

Khalid takes a step back. Satpal is now just three or four paces away and halts. Finishing his call, Satpal stuffs the phone back in his pocket. The two hold each other's gaze for a moment.

Khalid bridles but takes half a dozen steps back and stops, rolling up the sleeves of his kameez halfway up his forearm. His men stand behind him in a thick bunch.

Satpal smiles and takes deliberate steps towards Khalid, then spins on his heels and walks to the boundary wall that runs along the pavement. He leans his shoulder against the wall and places a call on his cell phone. Seeing a derisive grin on Khalid's face, he looks up to see a poster next to his shoulder asking, 'SUFFERING FROM WEAKNESS? CALL ...' Satpal shifts a bit to block it from view.

'Khalid Bhai,' Aslam whispers. 'One of our boys in the crowd just called me up with some news. It's not good.'

'What?'

'It seems two or three African students have been badly beaten up by the mob,' Aslam says. Khalid frowns. 'And some lunatics have dragged some women—'

'Women?' Khalid says with irritation, watching Satpal beckon Kultar as he talks on his phone.

'Some men have ... it seems that one of the women from that SUV has been gang-raped,' Aslam blurts out. 'The mob has formed a ring around that car.'

'Fucking sick dogs,' Khalid spits out. 'They should be castrated. But right now, Khan Chacha wants me to—'

'Bhai ... one of those two women is ... is Fatima,' Aslam says, eyes lowered.

'Those *bastards*!' Khalid hisses, turning to face him, his eyes flashing with rage. 'Where?'

'I was told it is happening behind the SUV,' Aslam says. 'We can't see it from here—there's too much crowd and other vehicles are also blocking the view.'

'Where are the children?'

'He ... the man who told me ... only saw Fatima being pulled into the mob surrounding the SUV. The children were not with her.'

'I have to get her out,' Khalid clenches his jaw. 'And the children. I will kill those bastards if anything has happened to Fatima.'

'But you said that Khan Chacha—'

'I know, I know,' Khalid interrupts Aslam. 'Listen, this is what I want you to do …'

77

'DCP,' Satpal mouths silently as Kultar approaches. The two lean in to hear the words on the speaker.

'—are stuck at the end of your street,' the deputy commissioner of police continues. 'Those two PCRs have only seven men—no weapons. So, they won't be able to help you much. But four squads of the anti-riot unit are on the way with water cannon and tear gas shells. They should reach within the next fifteen minutes. You just need to hold the crowd for a few more minutes. This is a huge mess.'

'Yes, sir,' Satpal says, straining to catch the DCP's words above the cacophony of slogans. He eyes the restless crowd that has now inched closer to the barricade.

'You know that Mehra's relative is the councillor there and he defeated Bashir's nephew in the recent elections,' the DCP states.

'Yes, sir.'

'And Bashir's cousin is head of the local unit of the ruling party in the state—and a legislator.'

'Yes, sir.'

'Have you understood what this means?'

'Yes sir,' Satpal sighs. 'It means I cannot put any blame on either of the two groups.'

'Correct. I heard what you told me, and I know what you think of them,' the DCP. 'But I want you to get promoted to an inspector's post this year. Your file is with me for final recommendation. Do you understand?'

'Yes, sir.'

'I do not want to get caught in a political crossfire.'

'I understand, sir.'

'I am getting flooded with calls from the media about what's going on there,' the DCP complains. 'They are fishing for news. The commissioner also got calls. Already, some channels are making wild guesses—some are saying it is political rivalry, others are hinting at communal aspects. They are pressing us very hard for a statement. I am sure the bloody vultures are hovering around, trying to get into the street. I have ordered the local units to block all entry and exit points. The street is locked down. You have to be very careful with what you tell reporters, if any get past.'

'Of course, sir,' Satpal rolls his eyes at Kultar who shakes his head in disgust at the sub-inspector's behaviour.

'It has to be as we discussed.'

'Yes, sir.'

'My secretary is typing out the statement I will shortly make to the media,' the DCP continues. 'So, let me hear what you will tell the reporters who you may come across there.'

'Sir, I will just stick to the story you have suggested,' Satpal says.

'I want to hear you repeat it,' the DCP insists. 'I want to be sure you got it right.'

Satpal clears his throat and looks at Kultar, indicating he too pay attention. Kultar steps closer to the sub-inspector.

'Sir, I saw some African students behaving rowdily in the market, disturbing the peace,' Satpal says. 'They roughed up and abused Bashir Khan—a senior citizen. They were probably high on booze or drugs. They—'

'Go on.'

'We don't tolerate such hooliganism, sir,' Satpal continues. 'I went to check on them a while later and found them drinking at the local pub and creating a huge racket. They had some other friends from the university who were all drinking—uh, even the girls. They—they looked suspicious—the way they were dressed. Questionable characters. I have noticed them at other times too—especially roaming the streets late at night. Not local girls—*outsiders*.'

'Hmm ... Go on.'

'I warned them and told them not to cause any trouble in the area,' Satpal says.

'What about the army chap?' the DCP asks. 'The Sikh?'

'He started arguing with me,' Satpal goes on. 'The Africans threatened me and said they would complain against me to their embassies. I tried to reason with them politely, but they ganged up against me.'

'Poor you, poor you,' the DCP says.

'The Sikh man ranted and raved against me and accused the police of brutality and harassment of innocent students,' Satpal says, warming up to his story. 'The fellow tried to physically intimidate me. Thinking it best not to escalate matters, I politely requested them to keep things calm and walked out of the pub.'

'A very rational and reasonable conduct,' the DCP croons. 'Then?'

'Next, I noticed them when a street fight had started between the students and some local men. The drunk students were blaming a couple of harmless autorickshaw drivers for allegedly molesting the girls. They caused a public nuisance on the street that led to an accident. A beggar boy was hit by a big SUV. Poor boy is badly injured.'

'What? Sir, you—' Kultar gasps. Satpal hushes him with a stern gesture and keeps talking.

'When the local people protested, the students and the SUV passengers ganged up and started beating up the auto chaps, vendors and other street folk. Probably, the students knew the people in the SUV. The SUV also had an African and a Northeastern woman—not a coincidence!'

The DCP clucks.

'And when my constable Kultar tried to intervene, the students and the SUV people turned on him. The crowd was angry and started retaliating. With great difficulty, Kultar and I apprehended some of the group and took them to the PCR. The crowd went berserk.'

'Very brave of you, Satpal,' the DCP says. 'So, basically, these students started all the mess?'

'Yes, sir.'

'And the SUV passengers ganged up with them?'

'Yes, sir,' Satpal says. 'Of late, we have got tip-offs about prostitution and a drugs racket in this area—mainly run by African and Northeastern students. Maybe the SUV people were the ringleaders. Sometimes, beggars and street vendors are used for peddling or pimping. Maybe the fight was about that. Of course, only investigation will bring the truth out.'

'Satpal,' the DCP says, sounding very pleased.

'Yes, sir?'

'It tallies with all the details that will be hinted at in my media release.'

'It was a spontaneous retaliation of the poor who are exploited by drug dealers and pimps who run this racket from the university. There is a strong indication of that, sir.'

'And our anti-riot squad will soon control things there with quick, decisive action.' The DCP's voice is grave.

'Yes, sir,' Satpal says. 'Just one request, sir ... can you get mobile networks to shut down in a radius of one kilometre? We don't want photographs or other distorted versions of the situation going viral. And completely lock down this area. We don't want any culprit to escape.'

'Certainly,' the DCP assures. 'Excellent suggestion. We will get it done immediately. Glad you have so quickly arrested the culprits.'

The line is disconnected and Satpal pockets his phone. Kultar looks at him with incredulous eyes.

'But, sir, I thought you wanted to teach Bashir Khan and Mehra—'

'This is only to make things easier for the DCP,' Satpal smiles. 'The trick is to first hit the least powerful. And manage the optics. I will hurt Bashir and Mehra through their stooges—Khalid and Bindal. Put them in for obstruction of police work and rioting. But a little later. For now, handcuff the students and the SUV women and put them inside the PCR. For the media, you know ...'

'Uh, we have only four sets of handcuffs and some rope.'

'Use them, Kultar, use them well,' Satpal says, strutting back to the PCR and the waiting group.

78

'Do you see these children?' Hari Shankar asks of the circle of women huddled near them. 'Do you feel nothing?'

They look back in silence.

'You are mothers yourself,' he continues. 'What would you have done if your kids were in a similar situation? Would you not have wanted someone to help? Do you feel nothing for their mother? No concern, no sadness, no anger? What kind of women are you?'

'It is not our fault,' a voice comes from the group. Then others chime in.

'Who asked her to go there?'

'Why was she so concerned about that black woman in the car that she abandoned her own kids?'

'She brought this upon herself. We know her—she always pokes her nose into things that don't concern her.'

'That's right. We have nothing to do with it.'

'I was here,' Hari Shankar screams. 'I saw it with my own eyes. I saw the way you looked at those crazy men—cheering them on and scaring them in the same breath. I may be old and frail, but I am not blind or deaf.'

'It was the men who did it,' a hawk-nosed woman in front says. 'They were going mad. How could we stop them?'

'We could do nothing,' a gnarled old woman said in a squeaky voice. 'We can do nothing. We are poor and we are women.'

'And you never feel like changing that? Standing united and drawing a line that men must not cross? Do you have no self-respect? No fight left in you?'

'That car ran over Fatima's brother,' the hawk-nosed woman said. 'They had to be punished.'

'There is the law for that,' Hari Shankar retorts. 'What they did to that foreigner woman … did she deserve that? Is that what you call punishment? Is this how any woman should be punished? Shame on you!'

'You are not a woman—you won't understand,' someone says.

'But you all are,' Hari Shankar says, shaking his head. 'And you feel what those men did is right?'

'We cannot fight everyone's battle,' the old woman screamed. 'She is not one of us.'

'And Fatima?' Hari Shankar asks. 'Many of you have seen her grow up on these streets.' There are murmurs of agreement.

'We remember when she came here with her mother, who sold flowers before her. You were here when Fatima's mother died of pneumonia during that cold December a few years back,' Hari Shankar says, seeking out known faces. 'Some of you helped her deliver this girl in Khalid's garage,' he continues, pointing at Nafisa. 'And I even remember some of you from that long and difficult night when Murad was born. We thought Fatima was going to bleed to death. You helped her. Do you not remember?'

Hari Shankar can see women shift on their feet, look at each other and nod their heads.

'So, is she also not one of us?' Hari Shankar asks, gesturing to include them all. 'We all struggle to survive on this street. Some of us live and sleep on these pavements. We eat and even cook here. We face the heat, cold and rains together. We laugh, we cry, we fight, we make up—all together in this little world of ours. Who else is there for us? And Fatima is *not* one of us?'

A sullen silence has settled all around.

'If you women don't stand up for Fatima today,' Hari Shankar says in a broken voice. 'If you do nothing for Fatima and those other women being mauled by those animals, you will never be able to forgive yourself.'

'We are not trash!' someone roars. 'He is right. Let's go, sisters.'

'We should go and get those women out.'

'Yes,' another voice joins in. 'And we will take them to the local clinic. The doctor madam is very good.'

The hawk-nosed woman strides forth and leans over the two children standing next to Hari Shankar. She bends down and pushes Nafisa's unruly locks away from her eyes and tucks them neatly behind the girl's ears. Nafisa frowns and un-tucks her hair back. The woman gives a tight smile and turns to little Murad and cups his chin in her palm momentarily. She looks over her shoulders at the bunch of women standing behind her. Her glinting eyes send a silent message and absorb reciprocal flashes and imperceptible nods. She gives Hari Shankar a hint of a smile and steps forward.

'Take Ali to the municipal clinic quickly, I know the duty doctors are still inside,' she instructs a few older women. 'I don't think anyone will stop you. The rest of us will bring Fatima and the other women there soon.' Five women lift Ali and lumber away.

'Follow me!' The hawk-nosed woman raises a fist and leads the remaining group of women towards the crowd surrounding the SUV. 'This feels a bit forced…!'

'Zindabad, zindabad!' the women take up the chant.

79

'Look, we have no choice,' Angad argues with Satpal. 'We have two women stuck in that crowd somewhere. Two students and a high-school boy are also trapped in that crowd. We can't just do nothing. My friend and her cousin are in there. I have to—'

'We have reinforcements coming. We need to wait for them,' Satpal says, holding up a hand. 'I have dealt with these kinds of mobs before. They are the worst. There is no reasoning, no agenda, just anger and hatred. You never know what triggered them and you can never guess what they will do.'

'Precisely,' Angad says. 'There are five women here. They need police protection. So, you cannot go. And you have just three other men in uniform with you. You need them with you to keep the mob at bay. I can take care of myself.'

'You can come with me,' Khalid says, walking up. Angad turns to the young man in the pathan-suit. 'I am going to get two children out of there, and their mother.'

'Who?' Satpal asks.

'Fatima's girl and boy are in there,' Khalid says. 'I hear Fatima has been ... is hurt. I have to get her out too. This chap can come with me if he wants. No one will touch me here.'

Satpal appraises Khalid for a moment. He can now hear women chanting 'zindabad' at a distance.

'Just what we needed,' Satpal sighs looking at Kultar. 'At least the stone pelting has stopped for now. Fine, soldier sahib, you can go with Khalid ... he is a local and knows his way around.'

'I will come too,' Titus says stepping forward.

'And us,' Karl says, nodding at Partho and Raunak, who don't look too comfortable with the suggestion. 'We will come with you, Angad.'

'No,' Angad says in a firm voice. 'We cannot all leave Uma and go. Besides, these policemen may need some help—there are just three of them. And that traffic constable. The same applies to you, Titus, my friend. You have to be with your friends here. My friend and I will bring your mates back.'

Titus looks at the scared faces of Faith and Sharon, and sighs.

'Okay,' he says. 'I guess that makes sense. Take care, bro—stay safe.'

Satpal has moved out of the discussion and leans against the PCR with his arms folded across his chest.

'Please, get Lorna back,' Malaika pleads from inside the PCR. 'And our friend Suraj.' Angad nods.

After exchanging quick fist-bumps with his friends, Angad follows Khalid away from the police car.

'Where are we headed?' he asks.

'I don't want to go towards the police barrier,' Khalid says over his shoulder. 'It will send a wrong message to the crowd. If we cross over from this side, they will feel free to cross over from that side. That flimsy metal barrier is just metal.'

'Makes sense, my friend,' Angad says. 'I am Angad Gill. I think you are a brave and good man. Thank you for helping us.'

'Satpal won't agree with you, that asshole,' Khalid grunts. 'I am Khalid. I have a small garage up there.' He points towards his garage.

'Who are these children you are going to get out?' Angad asks as Khalid passes his men and crosses the street.

'Oh, their mother is a poor flower-seller, who is like a sister to me,' Khalid says. 'Her mother was very kind to me when I started working in my foster-uncle's garage—may his soul rest in peace. And the girl delivered both babies in my garage.'

'Oh?' Angad nods, taking large steps to catch up with Khalid who weaves his way through the periphery of the crowd on the other side of the street. 'That is really nice of you, Khalid Bhai. We need that humanity in all this madness nowadays.'

Khalid gives a hollow laugh. 'I am not a believer in humanity,' he says as he elbows his way into the crowd. 'We will get into the crowd here as they seem quieter down this side. But you don't know anything about me, Angad Bhai.'

'I know a good man when I see one,' Angad says quietly.

80

The hawk-nosed woman pushes her way through the mob around the SUV.

The men turn around with irritated scowls. They take in the woman's thin lips, pock-marked face and hard, sunken eyes.

'Get lost,' a man snaps at her. 'This is no place for women.'

She holds the man's gaze and says nothing. Behind her, two wrinkled faces edge closer, their faded sarees fluttering in the hot breeze.

'This is exactly the place we need to be,' the hawk-nosed woman says. 'Make way.'

The two men stumble a bit, and the women make their way in. They hear grunts, groans and occasional laughter. Then there is a howl of glee.

The women emerge in a small, semi-circular vacant area around the black SUV. The men around are startled at the suddenness of their appearance. There is a hush.

Thoi is lying on her side, hugging her knees, head tucked into her chest. Her face is hidden in a disarray of straight, black hair, now caked in dirt. Her left sleeve is torn from shoulder down to her elbow. Her knee-length skirt is bunched up at the back, exposing her small buttocks. There are deep, bloody scratches all along her thighs and legs. Her shoulders shudder in arrhythmic spasms as her body tries to curl into a smaller space.

A few feet away, Fatima is on her back. A thick-set man with a bald patch is kneeling between her exposed thighs with his tight bush shirt pulled up above the bulge of his paunch. He is struggling to unbuckle the belt of his trousers. Her one eye is puffed and bruised. The cheekbone is swollen and black. Blood drips out of her mouth.

The hawk-nosed woman strides forward, grabs the collar of the man kneeling over Fatima from behind and pulls him up roughly. The unsuspecting man tumbles backwards to the ground just as he unbuckles his belt. The woman picks up a handful of dry dust and throws it in the man's shocked face.

As the man cries out in agony, the other women start kicking him. The man howls and curls up with his hands tucked between his legs. The men standing around cannot move and watch with gaping mouths.

The hawk-nosed woman steps away from the man and kneels down next to Fatima. She applies gentle pressure to Fatima's raised knees and straightens the girl's legs down to the ground. Then she pulls the hem of Fatima's kurta down to the knees. She turns and looks at the women who have come with her.

At an unspoken command, the women fan out and form a rough circle around Fatima and Thoi, including the whimpering man in their midst.

The old woman steps forward and picks up a piece of broken brick lying on the street. It is the size of her fist. She walks over to the whimpering man and looks at him for a long moment. Then, with a swift, deliberate move, she gets down on her haunches and smashes the brick on the man's upturned face. The whimpers change to shrieks. The old woman stands up and looks around. She beckons to another girl, who walks over in a trance-like gait. The old woman pats her shoulder and hands the brick to the girl who hesitates and looks at the circle of women around her with trembling lips. The old woman pats her on the back encouragingly. The girl nods back and draws a long breath. She raises her arm high above her shoulder, whips down from her waist and smashes the brick on the man's chest. Another woman follows and then another in a wild dance of retribution till the man moves no more.

A pair of women grip each of Thoi's arms across their shoulders, supporting her as she hobbles forward. They are followed by another pair of women carrying Fatima. Other women hover around them, now holding out a steadying arm, now caressing or making sounds of encouragement. As they walk, the surrounding men move away from their path, staring after them in silence.

The hawk-nosed woman stays behind till the last of the women have left. She is alone in the ring of men. The body of the mangled and broken man lies at her feet. No one utters a word or moves as she swivels her eyes from left to right. Briefly, her eyes rest on Lorna's lifeless legs dangling out of the car. She sucks in her thin lips and spits on the ground. Then, turning her back to the men, she walks away.

81

Khalid, Angad and the rest reach a point where the crowd is impenetrable. No amount of manoeuvring or jostling gets Khalid past the jumble of men and women, craning their necks to look at something going on up ahead.

'Stop, thief!' Angad shouts suddenly, pointing into the crowd. 'There he is—he took my wallet. There! I see him—make way, make way, please.'

A few people turn to look at Angad. They turn away, disinterested, but leave some space for him to pass.

'Brilliant!' Khalid whispers.

Angad grins. 'Thieves are universal enemies. People may not offer any help, but they let you pass.'

'I will remember that,' Khalid says with a laugh. 'Are you a student at the university?'

'I am in the army.'

Khalid keeps walking. He takes out his cell phone and tries to make a call. Shaking his head in disgust when he doesn't get through, he puts the phone back in his pocket.

'So, is your family from this town?' Angad grunts as he squeezes between a couple huddled around their two children. 'Excuse us, sorry.'

'No family,' Khalid says over his shoulder.

'But you said your garage belonged to your uncle.'

'Not real uncle,' Khalid says, walking sideways through the crowd. 'He found me roaming this street as a child and took me in. He was a religious man—a Haji. Never married. So he gifted me the garage on his deathbed. My religion is all that I have in my life,' Khalid adds after a pause.

'Khalid, that lamp-post to the left, ahead of you,' Angad pointing. 'The one with a banner hanging.'

'I see it. What about it?'

'I left that man in the crowd somewhere around here,' Angad says. 'Suraj. I promised to come back for him. He seemed injured. I had asked him to wait for me at the lamp-post …'

'That SUV hit Fatima's brother, Ali,' Khalid snaps. 'I have to find Fatima and her children.'

'The man is injured, Khalid,' Angad says, stopping and placing a hand on his shoulder. 'I am sure he did not harm Ali intentionally.'

Khalid doesn't move.

'*Allah helps the servant as long as he helps his brother,*' Angad says in a soft voice. 'I thought you were a religious man.'

'How do you know this hadith?' Khalid says, shocked.

'My ustad at the defence academy was a devout Muslim,' Angad says. 'We call our instructor "ustad". He told us never to leave one of our own behind in a battlefield.'

'That SUV fellow is not a brother,' Khalid objects.

'We are all on the same side,' Angad reasons. 'Against this crowd, aren't we? I am on your side. I want to help find Fatima and her kids. Aren't you on my side too?'

Khalid takes in Angad's earnest expression for a moment and sighs. He pats Angad's shoulder and heads for the lamp-post.

They find Suraj sitting on the pavement, clutching his right ankle. His face lights up in a disbelieving smile as he sees Angad. 'You came back for me?'

'Your friends are safe and waiting in the PCR,' Angad says, holding out a hand to help Suraj up. 'They are worried about you.'

'And Lorna?'

'We will find her too. But first, we must locate two little children and their mother for my friend Khalid here. Khalid, this is Suraj.'

Khalid rubs his beard. His face is grim and dark with anger.

'You ran over a boy I know,' he says.

Suraj takes Angad's support and hobbles a step or two and stands facing Khalid.

'It was an accident … I never meant to—'

'Of course, you never meant to,' Angad interjects. 'Khalid realizes that. That's why he is here to help you and together we will find Fatima and her children. The boy who got hit is her brother.'

'H-how old are the … they?' Suraj asks.

'What's that to you?' Khalid says, thrusting his chin out.

'I—my brother had a baby girl this morning,' Suraj shrugs. 'I became an uncle today.'

'Girl is five,' Khalid says, keeping his eyes on Suraj, who holds the gaze. 'The boy is barely two years old. Heard some men have taken Fatima and … we must find them.'

'So, what's the plan?' Suraj asks, limping past Khalid.

82

'Trust me,' Satpal says, placing his pistol back in its holster. 'This will help calm down those lunatics baying for your blood.'

'They're not baying for our blood, man,' Titus says. 'They're after you. *You* fired at them. They want *your* blood.'

'If that pleases you,' Satpal shrugs.

Titus looks at his handcuffs and tests how tight they are. Karl, Partho and Raunak have their hands cuffed as well. Kultar and Gulshan stand near the car's tailgate with a length of rope.

'I don't like this plan,' Raunak complains.

'Look—I'm telling you I'm a reporter with A2ZNews,' Karl protests. 'This is crazy!'

'You can't do this to them,' Uma says. 'They are not some cattle.'

'Listen up!' Satpal hisses. 'I have spent a decade in the force dealing with the madness of crowds. An angry crowd is like a pack of hungry hyenas. The only way to control them is by throwing them some morsels.'

'And we are those morsels!' Titus says sotto voce. 'Great.'

'Do you hear the crazed roar of that crowd?' Satpal asks. 'If you don't believe me, go stand closer to the crowd and see what happens.'

Titus exchanges glances with his fellow handcuffed men. He looks again at his cuffed hands, shrugs and takes measured steps to stand with his back against the vehicle.

'Titus,' Faith pleads. 'Come back here. You're exposed to any stones they throw!'

'The man is in uniform. He has a gun,' Titus shrugs. 'And I am handcuffed. I better do as he says.'

The other three men follow and line up along the side of the SUV. There is a perceptible drop in the volume of chants and slogans from the crowd now. Satpal gives the handcuffed men a crooked, smug smile.

'And now ... madams,' he says. 'Please cooperate with my men. It's your turn.'

'This is absolutely ridiculous,' Malaika says from inside the PCR. 'I will not be tied with a rope in—in front of that garbage crowd.'

'Well, madam ...' Satpal draws out his words. 'As our friend here just said, I am in uniform and I have a gun.'

There is an expectant lull around them. The crowd is watching them in near silence.

'Please, madam,' Kultar says, a coil of rope hanging from his shoulder. 'It is just for show. Boss knows what he is doing.'

'Yes, I do,' Satpal says. 'The crowd has seen us handcuff the men. They won't know how to react if they see us tie you also all up and bundle you into the PCR. Before they think of anything, we will drive away from here. Those men blocking the road to our left are known to me. They are trouble but they won't dare to stop us.'

'And then?' Uma asks.

'Once out of the crowd's sight, I will remove the handcuffs and untie you,' Satpal says with a small flourish of his hands.

'And we will head for the police station where we can sort out everything. Simple. The main thing is we have to get you out of here. Reinforcements will reach here any time now. They will control the mob.'

Uma takes a few seconds to decide and then, still hesitating, offers her wrists to Kultar. Gulshan helps tie a loose knot around Uma's hands and leads her into the PCR.

Uma gives Priscilla a nod of encouragement and Gulshan ties her hands up too. Faith and Sharon are also bound. They look at Malaika. With a snort of frustration, she lights up a cigarette and offers her hands to Gulshan. She sits with a defiant frown, puffing at the cigarette dangling from the corner of her mouth as Gulshan finishes his task.

There is a roar of approval from the crowd watching from beyond the barrier. Satpal looks at the handcuffed men with a knowing smile.

'And now, please get in with the ladies,' Satpal says. Then turning to Kultar, he adds, 'And pass that rope through their handcuffs. It will make for a good show for the crowd.'

The men do not resist when Kultar follows his orders. One by one, they scramble into the back of the PCR. Amit, the traffic constable climbs in last. Gulshan slams the tailgate shut. There is another cheer from the crowd.

The twin benches inside the PCR are meant to accommodate eight persons. The nine of them are cramped till Karl slides off the bench and sits on the floor, his back resting against the tailgate, facing Amit who is also on the floor with his back up against the driver row seats.

'I'll drive,' Satpal says and Gulshan hands over the keys. Kultar follows the aged head constable around the car and the two squeeze into the passenger bench.

'The street is clogged, sir,' Gulshan says, slamming his door shut. 'How will you drive out?'

'The pavement is not,' Satpal grins. 'We will take the pavement till Khalid's garage. After that, the street is clear.'

Ignoring the safety belt, Satpal turns the key in the ignition and starts the engine. As he adjusts the rear-view mirror, he sees Aslam march towards them with long, quick strides. Satpal releases the handbrake with a tired sigh but does not engage the gear. He taps his foot to rev up the engine a couple of times and waits.

Aslam leans down to the driver's window and grabs the frame. Satpal gives him a cold stare.

'You cannot leave,' Aslam says, glancing over his shoulder. His men have followed him. There are about half a dozen of them.

Satpal smiles and revs the engine again.

'We have to take the SUV people to Khan Chacha first,' Aslam continues. 'He wants them.'

'Why don't you take your mother and sister to him instead?' Satpal retorts. 'Maybe Bashir Khan wants them more.'

Aslam's eyes darken. His fist slams on the hardtop roof of the PCR. The metallic clang resonates in the confines of the car, making Satpal wince. Then another clang follows—louder and sharper.

Up ahead, one of Aslam's men clutches his head and drops to his knees. There is blood oozing from between his fingers. Realization dawns in Satpal's eyes and he shoves the gearstick, stepping on the accelerator. The car lurches and stalls. He curses and cranks the ignition key again. At the same time,

Aslam lunges through the window and grabs Satpal's collar with both hands. Around them, there is a hailstorm of bricks and stones.

'I will not let you go, motherfucker!' Aslam's eyes are clouded in rage, teeth bared in savage determination. He tightens his grip on Satpal's collar. The sub-inspector tries to say something but manages only to gasp and wheeze. Letting go of the ignition key, Satpal gropes at his belt, finds his pistol, pulls it out and fires through the window. He hears the women shriek. Aslam stumbles away, in shock. He falls down, as a blood wound in his stomach starts staining his kurta. Satpal starts the car, puts it in gear and presses down hard on the accelerator. The PCR leaps forward but Satpal has to jam the brakes to avoid ramming into Aslam's men, now frozen in the shower of brickbats.

With a loud crash, the windscreen cracks in a hundred jagged lines. Satpal screams, slapping his palms to his right eye. Behind him, he can hear the screams and moans of his passengers. He reaches gingerly for his right eye and starts as his fingertips touch the sharp edges of a shard of glass.

83

Junaid glares in cold fury at Bashir Khan and jabs a finger at the mayhem behind him.

'This—this cannot be tolerated,' he hisses. 'Look at what Mehra's goons are doing! We have to hit back now—hit back with vengeance.'

'Calm down, Junaid,' Bashir says, craning his neck to see what is happening. 'Aslam has—wait, he seems to be hurt. He's down ... I can't see him from here.'

'What is there to see, Khan Chacha?' Junaid asks through clenched teeth, his eyes blank with fury. 'Are you blind ... or deaf ... or just stupid?'

'Watch your tongue!' Bashir is incensed. 'You have to—'

'To what? Watch my friends being stoned to death?' Junaid shouts. 'We know Mehra has his men in that crowd—they are throwing stones at our boys. Aslam is hit! Two of our other boys have also been hit. Mehra's men stoned the van and our men. We have to retaliate. Now! We will burn those bastards with our petrol bombs.'

'Use your head, you idiot,' Bashir says. 'No one can see who is throwing stones from that crowd. But if you start anything, you and these boys will be in plain sight of that sub-inspector. He is sure to book us all for arson. We know how happy that will make him.'

'I don't care—I want Mehra's men to pay!' Junaid says. 'Wait till their stones are answered with our bombs.'

'I have seen what Molotov cocktails can do,' says Bashir. 'I saw it in Hazarajat where the rebels used it on Soviet soldiers. There are innocent bystanders here—people in vehicles trapped on the street. Think of—'

'Then why did you ask Khalid to stockpile the bottle bombs?' Junaid asks. 'For what? To shove them up our arses?'

'To be prepared for the worst-case scenario,' Bashir says. 'To be used at the right time.'

'Really?' Junaid asks. 'And what is that going to be? An Iftaar party? Or when our men are stoned to death? *When?*'

'When the Prophet—peace be upon him—was stoned out of the city of Ta'if, he restrained the angel Gabriel from crushing the wretched town under a mountain,' Bashir says, raising both palms to the sky. '*Our wrath must be directed to those who are throwing the stones—not every person on this street.*'

'There!' Junaid says, shaking with excitement. He points at two youngsters, even as one of them raises a brick and hurls it towards the PCR with practised ease. The brick lands with a sharp crack on the PCR's bonnet. His companion throws two stones in rapid succession. The second one catches one of Aslam's men in his back.

'There, Khan Chacha!' Junaid exults. 'Angel Gabriel has sent us a message. Now we know where the stones are coming from. The sneaky sons of whores!'

He turns and dashes into the garage. Moments later, he emerges holding a lit Molotov cocktail. His red-and-white chequered keffiyeh is now tied across his face.

Before anyone can react, Junaid runs down the pavement and throws bottle at the youngsters pelting stones. It is a long shot but the projectile hits the lamp-post and explodes in a meteoric shower of shards. Junaid turns back and raises both his fists in a gesture of victory.

'*Come on, friends!*' he gives an exultant yell.

Bashir looks at the scene in horror and turns around to stop the group intent on following Junaid, all carrying lit bottles. But they push past him, many armed with petrol bombs. Fiery missiles fly above the crowd of screaming men and women and smash into the area around the lamp-post. One of the bottles hits the lead man, and his clothes go up in flames as he hurtles through the crowd, shrieking in agony.

Several bottles land on the parked cars. Their passengers shout for help, unable to open their doors. Small pockets of fire erupt on all sides, trapping them. The crowd around the now-burning ice cream cart jostles to get away but is hemmed in by tiers of pressed bodies of equally panicked people. A car's fuel tank explodes, engulfing the people inside in flames.

84

Bindal gapes at the mayhem.

'Bastards of the devil!' Mehra bellows, gnashing his teeth. 'The time has come. Veeru, Sonu … go and tell Monty to start his attack. Today is a chance to destroy that den of Bashir's hooligans, once and for all. They have asked for it.'

The two assistants scramble away and Mehra turns his attention to Junaid and his mates standing in a semi-circle, eyeing their pyromania. Bashir stands under the tin awning of Khalid's garage with the remaining men like some general admiring his troops in a battlefield.

'He won't look so smug for long, understand?' Bindal whispers.

'Where is that halfwit Monty?' Mehra mutters. 'Hope he's not getting drunk in your basement.'

Bindal starts to speak but stops mid-sentence with a lop-sided smile etched across his face. 'They are coming out!'

Mehra glances over his shoulder. Monty steps out of Bindal's shop carrying two plastic buckets in each hand. He walks with light steps even though the buckets are filled with Molotov cocktails. Behind him, Veeru and Sonu hold two flaming torches of rags wrapped around short sticks. Mehra watches with approving eyes as Monty sets the buckets down on the pavement next to the monster speakers still blaring out bhajans. Gidwani puts a large plywood crate filled with bricks and construction stones next to the buckets. Bashir and his men are too engrossed in the sight of the burning car down the street to notice these preparations.

Monty's men fan out behind him as he picks up a bottle, lights the wick and aims the bottle across the street at Junaid and his group. The bottle smashes just short of where Junaid is standing. Junaid leaps away as bluish-orange flames fan out from the shattered bottle. There is a shout of warning from Bashir and several of his men run inside the garage while others react by picking up anything they can from the street and hurling them at Monty and his mates.

Unfazed by the onslaught, the men across the street light up more Molotov cocktails in quick succession and discharge a barrage towards the garage. Their actions are unhurried and coordinated. In turn, they prepare the lethal bottles, light them up and toss them at their target. They repeat the process with unflinching precision. Within a few seconds, the pavement in front of Khalid's garage is ablaze. Bashir, Junaid and the other men scurry about, dodging the burning missiles.

But Monty's dominance is short-lived. Soon, more men rush out of the dark interiors of the garage shed with flaring weapons of their own. They aim the first few at Monty and his band of men, then turn the trajectory to where Mehra and Bindal stand near the speakers. A bottle strikes one of the two speakers and instantly sets it on fire. Mehra curses and ducks, scampering to the relative safety of his shopfront, with Bindal close on his heels. The two peer out from behind a shutter at the scene unfolding outside.

At a command from Monty, a few of his men rush inside with the now-empty buckets while others grab brickbats and let loose a vicious attack, forcing their opponents to duck behind parked vehicles and the water tank outside the garage. The market area turns into a minefield of flames and smoke.

85

Khalid pushes through the crowd between the burning lamp-post to the left and a black Audi a few metres to the right. Angad is close behind him, with a supporting arm around the waist of a limping Suraj.

All around is absolute chaos. Screams of agony, cries of fear and yells of rage drown the senses. Men, women and children jostle about in panic, push, trip over each other and cry out in panic. Countless feet churn up dust, and pungent black smoke stings their eyes.

'I can walk on my own,' Suraj says, his breath a little short.

'I know you can,' Angad says. 'But we need to hurry up.'

'There they are!' Khalid exults. 'I see Hari Shankar with the kids under that tree to the right.'

Khalid races ahead, ploughing through the multitude with Angad and Suraj following in his wake. They reach the old man standing behind the gnarled trunk of a peepul tree soaring up from the pavement.

'Alhamdullilah! Thank you, Hari Shankar, for keeping the children safe,' Khalid says, grabbing the ice cream man's shoulders in gratitude and relief. 'Where is their mother? Where's Fatima?'

Hari Shankar looks at Khalid's wild eyes, then down at the two children hugging his legs. He shakes his head in sorrow and rubs the back of his hand across his eyes.

'I ... sh-she went into that crowd to h-help a woman ...' Hari Shankar fumbles. 'I-I tried to stop her. But you know how headstrong sh-she is. There was a group of m-men surrounding that car—one of the women from that car was ... the men were animals! Th-then they dragged another woman th-there. Fatima, she s-said ... she was so angry, I couldn't stop her. I am sorry, so sorry! I am old ... I-I wasn't ... someone had to take care of these children.'

'Waheguru!' Angad exhales. 'Do you know what happened to those women?'

'F-from here, I couldn't see,' Hari Shankar says, shaking his head. 'I can only s-see the roof of that car. But ...'

'What?' Khalid asks. 'But what?'

'Some women,' Hari Shankar blurts out. 'Harpreet was there ... you know the woman who heads the sweepers and who—'

'I know her,' Khalid snaps. 'She is the one who always fights with me about the grease and oil we spill on the pavement. As if she—'

'Yes, they went in to get F-Fatima and the other w-women back. I-I don't know what happened after that.'

'We must find out,' Angad says, starting to walk away. 'I promised to find the other woman who was in that car with Suraj. And then I have to look for my friends too.'

Khalid places a restraining hand on Angad and shakes his head.

'We have to take these children to safety first,' he says. 'Just look around you. I understand what you want to do. But please, I need your help. I will come back with you and Suraj to look for your friends—and Fatima. I promise.'

Angad casts a quick glance around. He hears distant crashes of glass and the whoosh of small explosions. The clang and clatter of falling stones from up the street is incessant. He looks at the little girl eyeing them expectantly, clutching her toddler brother's shoulders. There is a mixture of fear and determination in her dark, bright eyes.

Suraj takes a step forward and places a hand on her tousled, grimy hair.

'I am scared,' she says. 'Take me to my Ammi.'

'I will,' Suraj smiles back, patting her head. 'What's your name?'

'Nafisa. And this is my brother, Murad. I am older—much older.'

'There is a restaurant up the street,' Khalid says, looking over his shoulder with a worried expression as a brick bounces off the roof of a car behind them. The passengers trapped inside scream and try to break the windshield to get out. 'Khan Khana. I know the owner—he has a small office at the back of the kitchen. It is very secure. Let's first put these children there. It will take just a few minutes.'

Suraj looks at Angad with a nod and places an arm across Nafisa's frail shoulder.

'Okay, let's do this,' Angad says after a moment of thought. 'But after that, we come back to—'

'Yes, I promise,' Khalid says, picking up little Murad and seating him on his shoulders. He reaches out to Nafisa who continues to hold Suraj's hand.

'I will carry her,' Suraj offers, lifting the girl and placing her on his arms.

'Let me carry her,' Angad offers. 'Your foot is—'

'I told you, I am fine,' Suraj says. 'You walk ahead and clear the way for us. We need to hurry.'

'Follow us,' Khalid tells Hari Shankar as he leads the way. 'You look after these two in Bashir Khan's office while we come back for the others.'

Angad strides alongside Khalid, alert and vigilant. Suraj walks behind them, his face set tight as he carries Nafisa's small frame on his broad shoulders. Hari Shankar trails behind them, struggling to keep pace with the young men.

They walk in silence through the jumble of distraught men and women, avoiding pockets of smoke and sticking to the far side of the sidewalk. Tears well up in Hari Shankar's eyes as they skirt the burning ice cream cart and he halts in his tracks. A flaring bottle lands next to his feet with a loud crash, sending fragments of glass in every direction. The liquid inside splashes all over him, igniting his shabby clothes. He crumples to the ground, rolling on the hard flagstones, screaming in agony. Acrid kerosene flames confine him in a deadly ring of smoke and fire.

'Keep moving—don't stop!' Khalid shouts, shuffling sideways through the crazed horde. 'We can't reach him. There's nothing we can do for him. We need to get these children away first.'

The boy in Khalid's arms is bawling. His left cheek has a tiny cut, from which blood oozes out. His sister cries and tries to reach out to her brother but Suraj holds on to her tightly.

Angad swallows hard as he sees the thrashing figure of Hari Shankar wrapped in flames. He hears the children wail behind him and drags himself away from the spot.

86

The veins on Satpal's forehead are pronounced with the effort to control the pain he feels.

'Sir, you ... you are bleeding a lot,' Gulshan says in a hoarse voice. He casts frantic glances at the horde inching closer to the PCR.

'The crowd is coming this way,' he croaks. 'Let me drive, sir—they are almost at the barricade.'

Satpal spits out a stream of curses and turns his head to look behind. Two men have started pushing and pulling away the first traffic barrier. More rush forward to drag the connected rectangles of the Nadar barrier. A part of the barricade falls down and a loud cheer arises from the crowd. A few of them stamp on the fallen metal grills and break out in a dance.

'The bloody monkeys!' Satpal growls and pushes open the door of the PCR.

'I will teach them a lesson they won't forget.'

'Sir, don't!' Kultar and Gulashan cry out together.

'Get back in the car, sir,' Gulshan says, struggling to open his own door. 'I will drive.'

There is a bang as Satpal opens fire at the crowd. The sound is almost lost in the noise and the crowd continues to attack the barricade with unabated gusto. Satpal marches halfway down the intervening distance, takes aim at some man and fires again. The man continues to gyrate for another moment as if nothing has happened. Then blood spills down his forehead, dousing his face and shirtfront 'God help us,' Gulshan mutters under his breath, frozen in his seat.

A sudden lull descends on the crowd—but it is only for a fraction of a second. A blood-curdling roar rents the air as the rabble of men heaves forward, scrambling over the fallen barriers, kicking aside standing ones, screaming in unison.

Satpal takes a few hasty steps back and fires the remaining rounds of his pistol. As the inflamed mob bears down on him and the PCR, he tries to reload the pistol with his spare clip but is unable to do so as he stumbles on a brick and drops the magazine. The swarm is almost upon him, forcing him to turn around and make a mad dash for the PCR. He leaps back into the driver's seat and cranks up the window just as bodies slam into the side of the car. He slides home the central-locking catch on the inside and sits gasping for breath. He flinches as a face contorted in rage appears against the cracks in the windscreen. The man climbs atop the bonnet, banging on the glass.

'Killers!' he screams. 'You are all killers!'

Hands slam on Satpal's window and another face appears at it, teeth bared. 'You won't get away today,' the face screams. 'We will get you—each one of you.'

'You brought this on, you stupid man!' Malaika screeches from the passenger benches. 'Set us free! You will get us all killed, you arrogant bastard.'

'Sir, please let us drive away,' Kultar shouts. 'We can ram through these lunatics.'

Satpal's face screws up in agony. He turns the key in the ignition. The engine whines and coughs, then falls silent. He tries again with a prayer on his lips. This time, the PCR lurches forward a few inches, throwing off the man on the bonnet, and stalls.

87

With an impatient grunt, Mehra pushes back Bindal who is peering over his shoulder. He can see Monty and his boys pound Khalid's garage with Molotov cocktails and bricks. Bashir's men retaliate but Monty's side seems far better organized.

He can hear shots being fired near the PCR and a rising crescendo of angry shouts. The PCR is almost hidden from Mehra's view as it is now swamped with agitated men. Mehra's attention returns to Khalid's garage. They seem to be regrouping with a new strategy. The number of men throwing back petrol bombs seems to have reduced as many have gone inside the garage—perhaps to escape from Monty's hellfire.

Mehra turns to Bindal and smiles.

'Excellent, excellent! That's why I love Monty,' he exclaims. 'Just look at those sissies. Bashir is cowering behind the water tank and most of his men have scurried inside the garage. Even that psychopath sidekick of Khalid's, Junaid, is missing. The damage Monty has inflicted on the garage and the motorcycle and scooters of his clients will take Khalid months, if not years to recover from.'

'You are the mastermind of this,' Bindal chortles. 'Bashir will regret the day he fought with you after your uncle defeated his relative in the municipal elections, understand?'

'I have been itching to teach him a lesson—the stupid donkey from Kabul,' Mehra sniggers. 'I have told Monty to turn his attention to Bashir's filthy eatery after he finishes with Khalid's garage. They will both—wait, what's that?'

Mehra stops mid-sentence and points a finger at the garage. Masked men sally out rolling old tyres, charge past Bashir and let the tyres tumble away towards Monty. Some others hurl petrol bombs at the tyres, which explode in flames but keep hurtling towards Monty's men like great balls of fire.

'The treacherous swine!' Mehra gasps, face contorted in rage. He leaps out of his shop and waves both his hands, calling out to Monty who looks at him with an impatient gesture.

'Charge at them!' Mehra shouts over the pandemonium. 'Attack now! Kill them! Attack! Attack!' He gesticulates like a madman.

Monty says something to a couple of his cohorts wielding bamboo sticks. They race ahead and jab at the oncoming tyres with speed and dexterity. The foremost tyre spins off its path, wobbles and flips to the ground. The second one careens into the first and also topples to its side. The third one arcs around the defenders and ploughs through Monty's men who run helter-skelter from the wheel of fire.

Bindal yelps behind Mehra as the burning ring strikes one of the buckets holding kerosene-filled bottles. The bucket tumbles on its side and the tyre falls flat on the scattered bottles. There is a split second of silence, and then the pile explodes with a dull boom. Mehra covers his ears with his palms and screws his eyes shut against the flash of orange and heat that rises from the heap. A huge ball of smoke goes up and the surrounding pavement catches fire as the spilt kerosene spreads across it. A loud cheer goes up from the garage across the road.

Mehra ducks as he hears a shot. He sees Monty dart out of the smoke with a long knife glinting in the orange glow. Right behind him is Gidwani, his pistol raised above his head. Following them are others, armed with sticks, crowbars or knives.

Two rapid shots are returned from the garage and Mehra spots Junaid firing from behind the water tank. His men are carrying tools, motorcycle chains and broken bottles.

'Things are getting out of hand now,' Mehra hisses, pulling Bindal back towards the shop. 'You know the little door at the back that opens into the service lane behind the market?'

Bindal bobs his head several times, lumbering behind. His breath comes out in wet snorts as tears flow down his cheeks into his nostrils and blubbering mouth.

Right then, a Molotov cocktail shatters at Bindal's feet and engulfs him in a burning cloak. He screeches in shock and pain and tries to grab Mehra who runs away and ducks into his shop. Wheeling about, he grabs the collapsible grill and slams it shut against Bindal. Taking out a key from his pocket, Mehra unlocks the brass lock hanging from the latch and quickly slips it through the loop and locks it back. He takes a step away from the grill and watches the burning figure of his friend collapse on the ground, thrusting his flaming arms through the bars in a pitiable plea for mercy.

Mehra turns his head away and goes behind the cash counter. He unlocks the cash drawer and stuffs as much of the money as he can in his pockets. He sees the half-empty quart of vodka and grabs it before sliding the drawer shut. He takes a swig from the bottle as he throws one last look at Bindal, who is now slumped against the grill—still aflame.

Then he turns around and hurries to the back of his shop.

88

Bashir crouches and scutters away from the water tank, the spot where the attack seems to be focused. He heads for the entrance to the garage shed but hurries past it as Junaid peeps out and fires a shot at Monty's group. He finds refuge behind a metal piling supporting the far end of the shed's roof. There are a few aluminium trunks with spare parts piled up at the base of the piling and Bashir squats behind them.

He raises his eyes to the sky and murmurs a short prayer as a bottle bomb explodes right in front of the garage door. Junaid jumps back and vanishes into the garage. Bashir cranes his neck to peer over the top of the trunk. A battle is raging on the street. Men are pounding at each other with wrenches and crowbars, knives and screwdrivers.

Every now and then, a Molotov cocktail flies out into the sky, followed by a loud bang and more screams. While Junaid's men are mostly aiming at Monty's group spread out between Bindal's and Mehra's shops on the other side of the road, Monty's men occasionally also target Aslam's group still trapped in the crowd near the PCR. This earns a counter-attack of brickbats from that part of the street. Every moment, the battle is becoming more mindless with bombs, bricks and stones flying from all directions. There don't seem to be any sides anymore—just vengeful enemies everywhere.

Bashir spins around as he hears a whimper from behind one of the trunks. He duckwalks to the trunk and finds a lanky, dark boy crouching behind it. The boy sports a mohawk and his shivering upper lip has a soft fuzz that has yet to become a moustache. He is wearing a blue sports t-shirt over coordinated shorts. There are spots of blood on the front of his t-shirt and his left forearm is bleeding.

'Who are you?' Bashir whispers. 'You don't work at Khalid's garage.'

'T-Tom—Thomas Ku-Kurien,' the boy stammers. 'I live in the government colony behind this market.'

'What are you doing here?' Bashir asks, stealing a quick look above the trunk to ensure they haven't been spotted.

'I c-came to get my dad's s-scooter,' Tom replies. 'The h-horn wasn't working. I had left it here for repairs b-before the trouble started.' He looks apologetic.

'Why did you not go when ...' Bashir looks over his shoulder, '... when all this started?'

'D-dad had told me not to come back without getting the horn fixed.'

Bashir looks hard at the boy, but he doesn't look as if he were joking.

'So,' Tom continues, 'after leaving it here with the mechanics, I went inside the market to the bookshop. I love books.'

Bashir glares at the boy.

'I didn't hear any sound—I ... I was in the basement of the shop,' Tom blurts out. 'When I came up, the shopkeeper told me about the troub— ... the riot outside and asked me to wait till ... things settled down.'

'Then why didn't you wait?' Bashir asks. They both cringe as another shot is fired from somewhere close. A stone thuds on the trunk and clatters down.

'I waited for a while,' Tom whispers. 'Th-then the owner wanted to shut his shop. I had to leave. When I got out, the street was blocked and there was gunfire. I-I couldn't find a way out. Only when the crowd threw down the ba-barricade, I could get past. Th-then I was caught in all this fighting here and … my dad's scooter is parked here …'

Bashir narrows his eyes and scratches his beard. He takes another look at the battleground through a gap between the trunks.

'Where is your scooter?' he inquires.

'It's the la-last one … the Honda Activa with black—'

'I see it,' Bashir snaps. Then, he changes his tone to syrupy and smiles. 'Where is the key?'

'I gave it to the mechanic.'

Bashir groans and scowls at Tom as if he had committed a crime.

'B-but, I have a duplicate with me?' Tom says, with uncertainty lacing his voice.

Bashir pats Tom's cheeks with avuncular affection.

'Good boy, good boy,' he says. 'Do you want to get away from here, son?'

Tom nods several times.

'Then listen carefully, my boy,' Bashir says, placing a hand on Tom's head. He jerks a thumb over his shoulder. 'They are all engrossed in fighting. You move quietly to your scooter—'

'It's my dad's scooter,' Tom reminds.

'Your dad's scooter,' Bashir agrees, clenching his jaws. 'Get on it and start it. I know a—'

'But the horn isn't fixed yet, I think,' Tom objects.

'The hor—' Bashir hisses, then corrects his tone. 'Listen carefully, son. For now, the rioting is only up to this part of the street. This garage marks the outer limit of the violence. But we can see the mob has already surrounded that PCR. Very soon, it will overflow in this direction. That horde cannot be contained anymore. It will destroy everything in its path, including your—uh—your father's expensive scooter. Do you understand?'

Tom nods and casts a worried look at the scooter.

'Right now, the rest of the street ahead of this garage is quiet and empty,' Bashir points a finger. 'I can guide you out of this place. I know a back alley through which we can circle back to your colony. You will be safe and your … father's scooter will be safe. The horn can be repaired another day at some other garage. Do you want me to help you?'

Tom nods again.

'Smart boy,' Bashir croons. 'Now go and start the scooter and wait for me. The moment I join you, drive like crazy out of this mess. Now go!'

Tom doesn't move. His eyes are fixed at the garage entrance where oil patches are smouldering and flames are creeping up the wooden door jamb.

'Go, go, go!' Bashir hisses. 'They are all fighting on the other side of the street now. Hurry.'

Tom gets down on fours and scuttles towards his dad's scooter parked along the pavement, a few metres away.

Bashir licks his lips and watches him with a look of relief and anticipation.

Tom mounts the scooter, slides it off its stand and starts the engine. The soft purring noise is drowned in the sound of the raging riot—the crashes, the screams, the roars, the crackle of flames and thuds of falling stones.

Tom pushes the two-wheeler with his legs to face up-street. He turns to look at Bashir and nods.

Bashir closes his eyes and touches the tips of his fingers to his eyelids. Then he springs up and races to the scooter. He clambers on to the pillion seat and thumps Tom on his back. The boy revs the engine and speeds away.

89

Still running, Angad spots something. He shuffles with lightning speed and gets up close to the man about to bring down the steel curtain rod poised high above his head for the downswing. The man did not expect this counter-intuitive move—instead of moving away, the crazy Sikh closes the gap. Angad jabs the man's chin with a brutal upper cut. As the man staggers back, Angad delivers a powerful kick to his stomach, sending him flying across the pavement.

'Come on,' Angad beckons Khalid and Suraj. 'Let's keep moving. I can handle them.'

Suraj picks up a rod and follows the other two with Nafisa clinging to him. Khalid is still carrying Murad in his arms.

They jog close to the shopfronts to their right, which are either shuttered or abandoned. A few are burning. The two men carrying the children take care to give the flames a wide berth as they run past. Angad covers them from the left, acting as a shield against any threat from the middle of the street, where the action has now moved.

There are battered or burned bodies lying all over the pavement and the street. There are a few small groups of men scattered along the sides, throwing stones, chasing others and exchanging blows. On either side, groups huddle around stockpiles of Molotov cocktails. There seems to be no specific target anymore nor anyone giving directions. Men are hurling bombs at whatever takes their fancy.

Angad steps forward as he sees a man break away from his group to come charging at them with a broken bottle. Another man follows him, waving a hacksaw.

'Look out! That is Khalid,' the man with the hacksaw shouts at the man leading. 'The gang leader of Bashir's goons. Let's get him!'

The man with the broken bottle lunges at Angad, who is prepared for him. He manages to push him away, narrowly missing the jab of the broken bottle.

The second attacker veers around and rushes at Khalid.

Suraj hobbles forward holding his rod and swings it in an upward arc. The tip slams the attacker's cheekbone with a sickening crack, drawing blood. The man staggers and screams in pain. His eyes are white with fury and he swings his hacksaw in a wild arc, leaving a thin, wet gash across Suraj's black t-shirt.

Nafisa remains clinging to his back, unharmed—except for a little splash of blood on her frock from Suraj's wound.

Angad breaks the man's elbow, as the opponent lets out a cry of pain. Angad purses his lips in satisfaction.

He jerks his head up at the bang of Khalid's pistol. The man with the hacksaw attacking Suraj buckles to his knees, then falls on his face with his hands twisted under his belly. A dark pool of blood creeps out from under his chest.

'Leave that man!' Khalid shouts waving his pistol. 'Their mates will come for us. I can see Bashir's restaurant is on fire—so, we can't take the children there. But the next shop is Mehra's—the one with the shutter closed and ... and that dead man lying across it. There's a small door at the back that opens on to the service lane behind the market.'

Angad walks over with an expression of revulsion and drags the body a few feet away. Its face is charred beyond recognition. He holds his breath against the stench as he heaves the heavy corpse.

Khalid and Suraj keep an eye on the men fighting on the street. They exchange worried glances as they notice some of the men looking towards them and pointing.

'Hurry up,' Khalid says, holding his pistol ready.

'The shutter seems latched and locked from inside,' Angad says as he tries to pull the grill open.

Suraj gently puts Nafisa down on the pavement and slides his rod into a small gap between the dual shutter panels and leverages it against the latch. With a mighty heave, the panels crack apart as the latch gives way. With a grin, Suraj pushes the panels further to create a gap big enough for a man to pass through. He twirls his rod, which is now slightly bent in the middle.

'Listen, this man—uh—Suraj and I will stand guard here,' Khalid tells Angad, putting Murad down on the ground. The boy runs to his sister and wraps his arms around her. 'You take the children inside the shop and find the rear door. It will probably be locked, so break the lock.'

'But, if we attack, those men will come after us,' Suraj says, eyeing the men on the street regrouping and forming an attack team. 'This grill can't be locked now.'

'Nafisa, listen carefully,' Khalid bends down to look the girl in her terrified eyes. 'This uncle will show you the door at the back. Take your brother and run away. We won't let anyone reach you. We will come for you afterwards.'

'Ammi?' Murad squeaks. Nafisa hugs him tighter.

'You run,' Khalid says. 'Me and these uncles will go and get your Ammi later. Understand?'

Nafisa nods and allows Angad to hold her hand and take her into the shop. The little boy toddles along with them. Angad walks past the cash counter and the shelves lined with garments. He pushes open a swing door that leads to a small storage area with tall racks of cardboard boxes filled with a variety of fabrics and garments.

'Ammi?' The little boy starts to cry.

'You are a big boy now,' his sister tells him. 'We have to follow this uncle. Khalid Mamu will bring Ammi to us.'

Angad turns and pats the girl with a reassuring smile. At the far end of the storeroom there is a toilet to the left and a narrow passage to another door. The barrel bolt at the top of the door is down. He pushes the panel with his fingers and the door creaks open. There is a narrow, empty lane outside with the backs of buildings lining either side.

'Look, I am going back to bring your Khalid Mamu here. If I don't return in five minutes, you go out of this door with your brother and latch it from outside, behind you. And do not come out to the shop, no matter what. Understand? Now repeat what I just told you.'

Nafisa repeats everything Angad said. He grins and pats her cheek.

'Do you understand what's five minutes?' he asks, a thought striking him. Nafisa shakes her head.

'Umm, it is as much time as you would take to ... to ... uh ... to ...' Angad is at a loss for words.

'To eat an ice cream?' Nafisa asks.

'Brilliant!' Angad exclaims. 'You are the brightest girl I know! Yes, in that much time, if I, Khalid Mamu or the other uncle who carried you don't return, then just run and hide somewhere. Promise?'

Nafisa nods. Angad ruffles her hair with a smile.

Distracted by the sudden shouts from outside, Angad bolts the door behind him and hurries back into the storeroom. Nafisa looks at the secured bolt that is too high for her to open. She looks about for any box or furniture she can use to climb up to the bolt but finds none. She turns around with a worried look as she hears the swing door to the shop slam after Angad. Walking up to Murad, she pulls him close.

90

Satpal tries to open the door but the swarm of bodies against it makes it impossible to do so.

'Don't open the door, sir!' Gulshan begs. 'This crowd will lynch us.'

The mob on his side push and those on the driver's side start pulling.

'I have to try talking to them,' Satpal shouts. 'There are consequences to obstructing the police.'

'Consequences?' Malaika's shrill voice comes from behind. 'You retard, you think they care for consequences? Did you think of consequences before you fired at them or dumped us here? I will file a case against you.'

'Shut up, you spoilt bitch!' Satpal cries. 'You think they like you more than they like us? If I don't talk them down, they are going to—'

'Listen, man, just cut us loose,' Titus pleads. 'We will try to reason with them. They hate you more right now. First you shot at them and now you have probably run over someone. You don't stand a chance outside. Listen to your man—stay inside till the mob calms down a bit. And let us out.'

'He is right,' Uma says. 'There are five women in here. We will step out first. Let us talk to them.'

The thumping from outside gets more frenetic.

The car begins to rock a little. Outside the windows, on the driver's side, they can only see dozens of pulling hands. The women scream.

The rocking movement of the PCR gains momentum as countless hands push against it and shoulders heave and strain. The screams from the passengers become louder. Satpal cranks the key several times and stomps on the accelerator pedal. The car refuses to start.

'Gulshan, don't!' Satpal shouts as his subordinate leans over the seat with a pocket knife and tries to cut the rope binding the nine prisoners.

'Sir, we have nothing to lose,' Gulshan responds. 'Maybe the women are right.'

'The crowd will devour them,' Satpal cries. 'Stop!'

The knife slips from Gulshan's fingers as the car teeters at a dangerous angle. Screams and shrieks fill the air inside. The seesaw motion increases in amplitude and the crowd lets out a victorious roar. Satpal holds the steering wheel tight while his subordinates knock about, bumping into the window and the dashboard.

Metal screeches, nuts and bolts creak. The fissures on the windshield deepen. Satpal's head bangs against his window making him groan and his sunglasses fly off. The car lurches to an impossible angle and freezes. With inexorable slowness, it starts to lean over to the driver's side, inch by agonizing inch.

Someone kicks at Satpal's window and it shatters. He reaches out his hand to grab the collar of the man outside. The PCR passes beyond the point of no return and crashes on its side, trapping Satpal's outstretched hand under it.

A victory cry goes up from the mob. People clap and embrace each other in unholy glee. A trickle of diesel oozes out of the fuel tank underneath and makes a puddle. A scrawny, tall man steps forward and waves the crowd away. He stands with his feet planted wide apart and fishes out a cigarette. He strikes a match with a flourish and lights the cigarette. Stamping out the lit match under his scuffed sneakers, he smiles at the men gathered around him, ignoring the cries for help from those trapped inside the PCR.

The man takes a few languorous puffs and waves the crowd further away from the PCR. Sensing something about to happen, the jostling men retreat, leaving a large, empty circle of open space around the man and the overturned PCR. The man picks out a few matchsticks in his right hand and holds the box in his left. He raises both his hands high above his head and shows them to the crowd, like a magician about to perform a neat trick. There is a murmur of anticipation from the crowd. He puts the burning tip of his cigarette to the matchsticks, lighting them up and hurls them at a pool of diesel.

Flames fan out with a dull blast, setting the tyres on fire. Within moments, the rubber parts are aflame and the paintwork gets pockmarked with heat bubbles. The undercarriage bursts into flames with a big explosion, enveloping the whole car.

91

Angad hurries as he hears a shot fired from the shopfront. He bursts out to find Khalid slowly swinging his pistol in front of him from side to side, facing half-a-dozen men armed with a variety of makeshift weapons. Next to Khalid, Suraj sways his bent curtain rod, poised to strike if anyone moves close.

Angad takes up position behind them and scans the ground for anything he can use as a weapon. He finds nothing, so he pulls the grill shut and stands at the entrance, arms akimbo.

For a brief moment, no one seems to move. The attackers and the defenders appraise each other and wait for someone to break the impasse. A curly-haired man in a flowing orange kurta wielding a hammer exchanges glances with a man who has his face wrapped in a green keffiyeh, brandishing a motorcycle's exhaust pipe. They nod at each other, space out and charge.

Khalid takes aim and shoots the masked man who spins and drops to the ground. Suraj strides forward and sinks to the ground, sweeping with his curtain-rod to bring down the man in the orange kurta. In one fluid motion, he changes his grip and smashes the rod down on the man's head.

The rest of the assailants explode into action and swarm in from every direction. Khalid pulls the trigger but his gun is jammed. He tries again, with no result. Before he can react, a swarthy man cannons into him with a broken bottle that he drives deep into Khalid's stomach. Khalid groans and staggers back. The attacker thrusts the bottle deeper and wrenches it upward. Blood pours out of the mouth of the bottle and Khalid falls to the ground.

Suraj fights with his rod like a man possessed, till one of the assailants hurls a brick that hits him in the temple, smashing half his face in. He slumps to the ground without a sound. He lies there, eyes glazed, chest shuddering, his breath coming in ragged gasps. His limbs twitch for a few moments before going still.

Angad throws punches and kicks but is gradually beaten back to the entrance. He is hammered, cut and jabbed till his feet falter and his vision blurs. He sinks to the pavement, still blocking the grilled doorway with outstretched arms, his forearms hooked through the slats in the panels. There is a blizzard of rocks and bricks from the left, strafing the attackers. The crowd is on a rampage after burning down the PCR and the last vestiges of law and order have vanished. The attacking goons turn on their heels and run up the street to escape the approaching horde. Angad weaves his fingers through the grill bars and holds them in a death grip. His head lolls back against the grill and blood drips down his nose and mouth, soaking his white shirt in red.

The herd of people seeking only death and destruction run past the shop, chasing after Mehra's and Bashir's gangs. Their faces are contorted and eyes blank in single-minded pursuit.

No one seems to be leading them—it is a flowing river of violence. Angad watches them through blood-coated, puffed eyes. They pay no attention to the pile of men lying around the shopfront and lope away. A pained sigh escapes Angad and his head sags down on his chest.

PART THREE
Consumed

92

Hari Shankar tries to blink away the drops of sweat stinging his eyes.

There is no feeling in his arms, no strength left in his legs. It is hot and suffocating. The smoke is rancid, with the smell of burning flesh. Or is it the stench of combusting humanity?

It takes such little effort to set humanity on fire, he thinks. The burning is instantaneous. Sometimes, spontaneous. Humanity melts, peels off, twists and goes up in smoke. There is so much hatred packed inside, that a sound, a sight, a touch, a thought can set it aflame. You just have to scratch the skin to find the raw, dry cinder inside hollow souls.

There are varied forms and textures of that cinder.

But they burn everything. Outside burn; inside burn.

They burn young boys who laugh, sell books, eat ice creams and refuse to be burdened by the weight of life. They incinerate girls who love their mothers and take care of infant brothers. They singe mothers. They suck women into searing furnaces powered by insatiable lust. They consume the different, the resisting, the protesting, the questioning. And they set ablaze the meek and the compliant. They sear the arrogant and they set fire to the humble. All of it hurts. But it hurts the most when they burn hope. The hope of a better life, of happiness and of peace. The hope of an ice cream seller trapped hundreds of miles away from his home and family. The hope of getting a daughter married off, of seeing a son thrive in a good job and of seeing a satisfied smile on a partner's face.

Will things ever change?

Will this inside burn ever cease?

Hari Shankar's breath quickens. He can hear his heart thudding in his ears. *And me? What about my burn? I hope it doesn't destroy my soul.*

A voice speaks from inside: do not worry about your soul.

Weapons cannot cut It, nor can fire burn It; water cannot wet It, nor can wind dry It.

93

Fatima looks up from the hard, plastic-sheeted bed at the cobwebs on the white ceiling of the room. The walls around her are dark green.

It has been a while since she has felt the comfort of a bed underneath her. The pavement was so much harder. The last time she was on her back, looking up at the ceiling, her knees had been slightly bent and legs spread. She remembers the dry, dull pain as fingers pried and prodded between them. She can feel it again. Only this time, the pain is sharper but the fingers exploring are soft and gentle.

Of course, the last time, there were no tubes running from plastic bottles hung from hooks on a steel rod, piercing blood vessels, making her arms throb. There was also no stinging sensation as parts of her she never wants to look at again are dabbed and cleaned.

The searing pain subsides and she can think again. Why does she always do the wrong thing? Why does she reach the wrong place at the wrong time, every time? Is it God who makes this happen? Surely, that cannot be. Because her God is all merciful. And there is only one God. And she prays to Him five times every day. What has she done wrong?

Is it a sin to be born on the street? To grow up without knowing the love of parents? Is being hungry wrong? Is being a woman a crime against humanity? Only God knows the answers to these questions—she cannot fathom them.

People have accused her of having desires and aspirations. Indeed, she is guilty of that. She longs for a soft bed, clothes that do not expose her skin or stink and hair that can be combed more easily. She wants a watch. Not that time matters when life is one long, uninterrupted and unending period of deprivation and denial. People buy flowers from her to give to someone they love. She aches for someone to give her a flower too, someday.

She wants a future for Nafisa and Murad. She wants them to learn to read and write. Maybe even have an egg or two every week. She would like a prince to come and take Nafisa away in a shiny, white car to marry her and pamper her in a vast palace of four rooms with two servants. That would be divine.

She prays for Murad to grow fat, so that his little ribs stop showing. She wants to see him grow big, tall and handsome and become a businessman like Hari Chacha. Or maybe even own an autorickshaw taxi. She has heard from Ramji that they earn fifteen thousand rupees a month, sometimes even twenty. Imagine the life of absolute luxury she could have in her old age, if Murad were to drive an autorickshaw.

And Ali? Her poor brother. He is holding on. The good doctor of the clinic has assured her. She thinks he will be all right. Fatima is happy to have him in the next bed. He cannot talk but is conscious. That's what the lady doctor says. She knows he has it in him to be successful in life. Hari Shankar agrees. Ali goes to night school when he can. Maybe he will become a police constable when he grows up. How much power he will have then! And she and her children will have nothing to worry about.

She wonders where the children are. Hari Shankar is like a grandfather to them. They were safe with him. She wishes she were less groggy, and tells herself she will go and find them as soon as she can walk.

And she will love them.

If she lives.

94

Thoi tries not to scream as the thick needle squeezes what feels like oil into her buttock. The anti-tetanus shot was far less painful. Her senses are fading, but her head is squirming with thoughts.

Will things ever be the same? What about her life? How long it had taken for Angad to express his feelings for her … They had liked each other for a while, but he had told her on graduation night, just after their twelfth-standard board exams. They had danced through that evening.

But will he feel the same for her now? How could she blame Angad if he started to feel different after what those horrible men did?

What will Mama and Pa say? How will they feel? Will they understand what happened today? Will they be angry? Ashamed? No, it is not possible for life to be the same hereafter.

And what about Bonium? The poor boy has no future anymore. Only a past. A past that ended in dirt, amidst blood, drool and flowing urine as his mind lost control and his body could take no more of the hate. What was *his* crime? He wasn't even a woman. Nor yet a man. How does it feel to die on a day you woke up thinking you are immortal? That death is what happens to old people with bent bones and wrinkled skin. That life holds infinite possibilities. What went through his mind when he was being kicked? That the next breath would be his last? That he would never feel the tender touch of his mother's fingers running through his unruly hair? Or hear the warm, strong voice of his father calling out his name? That he would never know the love of a woman?

Life—even a cracked and battered one—is better than the final intactness of death.

She has been told so often that forgiveness is the gateway to redemption and peace. That it heals and brings one closer to the Lord. Maybe praying helps.

And when you stand praying, if you hold anything against anyone, forgive them, so that your Father in heaven may forgive you your sins.' **Mark 11:25**

But it doesn't help. Other thoughts, vivid images invade her mind. Of gouging, clawing, stabbing, slicing, maiming, killing.

O Lord! There would be so much to deal with in the world outside this green clinic.

95

The steel body of the PCR does not burn but gets hotter by the second, baking the very air inside. It is like being cooked in a tandoor, Satpal thinks.

Strange, but his hand stuck outside still has some sensation left in it. It feels so much cooler. The fingers do not respond to any command from the mind but they catch the breeze outside the inferno and tingle. An antenna of life.

And what a life it has been. Growing up under the hard hand of a father who never learnt when to stop. Anything. Eating, drinking, beating ... even loving. The dreaded 'encounter' specialist that he was, he just couldn't stop killing. He believed in a wild kind of justice.

It was on the day after his father's funeral that Satpal's mother suggested he join the police force. She felt police work had a future. She thought it was the most suitable job for her son. Maybe she wasn't wrong.

The decade as a sub-inspector has been good. There is a recommendation for him to be promoted to the rank of inspector. The number of his 'encounter killings' in the first ten years, not including today's count, almost equals his father's. Maybe that was why he is being 'cooled off' for the past four months in a routine posting outside the Crime Branch.

It has been smooth sailing mostly, at work and in life. Except for his marriage. That turned out to be a disaster. That's what comes of marrying too much above oneself. His wife thought being a receptionist in a star-rated hotel was somehow superior. It hadn't taken many years for their initial lust to boil down to tolerance, which too evaporated quickly, giving way to viscous distaste and then granular hatred. Their only daughter was just five when her mother left and took her away. Eight months have gone by since, but the sense of loss remains. A nagging, hurting, empty feeling of loss, befuddlement and betrayal. And, above all, of being powerless. Just like he felt when the overturned PCR caught fire. Here he was, about to be crushed and burnt, with this empty gun stuck in his holster.

Fully loaded, a gun makes a big difference. The awareness of carrying death slapping against the thigh is a heady feeling. It makes everyone around seem smaller and weaker. And the uniform ... Together they don't help to win hearts. But snatching bodies, yes.

Walking into that pub just about an hour back didn't foretell collecting so many bodies today. Especially these young women now turning to melting flesh. All weaker and smaller, yet trying to act so big. But they were put in their places, weren't they? Right in the back of the PCR, their hands trussed up. And now getting incinerated.

This insane crowd. A beast. There was nothing wrong with firing the first shot. Or the second. Or the one after that. Every experienced policeman knows that a mob doesn't have two things: a head and balls. If it tries to grow either, shoot it. Strange, it did not work today. Maybe because the mob today was like an amoeba. Unicellular: just a palpating mass feeding on and excreting violence.

What was so different today? A beggar hit by a car driven by the rich. Some wailing and shouting on the street. The usual gravitation of the dregs, always looking for an opportunity to vent their anger against hunger, deprivation, subjugation and greed. Always failing. The losers. On any other day, they could be threatened, cajoled, fooled ... or shot. And they would take it. But what happened today? What triggered this uncontrollable mob? What brought about the metamorphosis from an amoeba to a tyrannosaurus? It makes no sense to Satpal.

Dying as a full-fledged inspector of police would have made sense. Leaving behind a higher pension for his daughter would have made sense. Making a dramatic escape after a shootout would have made sense. Getting a gallantry award would have made sense. Just killing a magazine-full of people would have made sense. Saving the poor wretches tied up behind would make sense.

But this ... Being trapped in this stupid, battered PCR makes no sense. Having a gun without bullets makes no sense. That fancy-pants woman begging for mercy makes no sense. Saying sorry to no one in particular makes no sense. Feeling remorse makes no sense. Wanting to make things right makes no sense.

Death by fire makes no sense.

96

Malaika looks at the little flames crawling up her grey slacks like fiery worms. She tries to pull her other leg out from under a body—God knows whose! Her face screws up in pain and she falls back. It is impossible. She tries to lift herself sideways. If she can push her bound wrists towards the fire, maybe the rope will burn off. As if playing with her, the flames dodge her extended arms and creep along the back of her right thigh, making her scream. She almost blacks out.

Thoughts collide and memories flash past inside her head making her dizzy. So many people say she can keep a cool head and think out of the box. It is difficult to keep a cool head when your hair is on fire. Or think out of a burning coffin. The smoke is suffocating.

Of course she had a cool head. Instead of joining some big firm after her fashion designing course, she chose to start her own boutique selling designer partywear. People had warned her about the stiff competition, but she thought she knew better. When the banks foreclosed her loan, her mother wanted her to join the family in Canada. As if Mom cared! Ever since she'd divorced Dad fourteen years ago, Mom had never come to India.

Malaika had kept a cool head.

It was she who had made annual summer trips to Canada till she graduated from college. Thereafter, when she went to the fashion technology institute, she stopped going. That was six years ago. Canada! And who would have been with Dad while he slowly lost his mind to Alzheimer's? That had made her furious.

But Malaika had kept a cool head.

That was four years ago. Abandoning design, she'd moved to fabric sourcing. It was hard, energy-sapping work—finding clients, scouting for exotic prints and weaves, bargaining. Her tenacity and grit paid off. Two years back, she finally started a small company of her own, specializing in supplying hand-woven silk and cotton to high-end designers from Europe.

It has been a tough and lonely road to success. And just as she has started to enjoy the fruits of her labour ... this is what happens. The world goes up in flames.

Coming back to her senses, Malaika feels scorching pain spreading across her thighs and lower back. The heat source above her head has moved in closer, singing her hair, producing a sharp smell. If only she could move a little. Maybe roll over the flames to smother them. But you cannot roll over if your leg is trapped under a cadaver and the other is on fire. You cannot move when both your hands are tied up with a thick rope that refuses to burn off. You cannot move if the relentless blaze all around is taking off your eyelashes and eyebrows.

A hand reaches out for her and she screams for help. Surely, they will pull her out of this hell now? She stares at the hand hanging close to her head, doing nothing. *Pull me out!* She sobs loudly. *I don't want to die! Please.* The hand rotates slowly in the air. She watches it with hope, then worry and finally with horror as it turns a full circle and drops down on her—a lifeless stub of charred flesh and skin. This time, Malaika cannot hear her own scream.

97

Suraj feels numb, like suspended in nothingness. He can only open his right eye. All pain has receded just as the world around him is fading away. He can only see the brown sky, covered with dark grey clouds gathering above him. It is not easy to breathe with so much blood flowing up his nasal passage. He has to breathe through his mouth. His eyelids droop, and he wills them open again. The clouds are talking to him, making wondrous shapes, changing shades. Now that one looks like a heart.

So much love will go to waste.

The cloud is a face with a wry smile. *Her* face!

It was a mistake to defer the marriage till she finished college the next year. She had proved that there was something called love at first sight. From the moment she had walked in with her parents, Suraj knew he could not live without her.

The cloud gathers into a soft lump that droops down with pity.

Suraj had forgotten about his quarrel with his father about an arranged marriage the moment he saw her. As such, he forgets all quarrels with his father in the end. Papa dotes on him. He is the youngest of two sons—a rare privilege indeed. Mummy is a step ahead of Papa. She considers him a divine gift from her gods: a boon for years of prayers for a second son. She is deeply religious. Her sons consider her their religion.

The cloud forms into his mother's soft, round face with two large eyes and a pug nose. Sunrays filter through her loving smile and cover Suraj in warmth.

Maybe, so much love and adoration make a person smug and selfish. Maybe it breeds a sense of entitlement that encourages a person to push, snatch, demand and resent. As if the universe owes him whatever he wants. And if someone comes in the way, the hurdle has to be smashed away.

The cloud flares out like a slow-motion explosion.

But one cannot get everything one wants. Most of his friends have sisters. Suraj just has a brother who is so much older that he behaves like an indulgent uncle rather than a competing brother. Suraj has always missed having a sister. He feels sad on the festivals of rakhi and bhai-dooj with no sister to tie a glittering rakhi on his wrist or put a big, red tika on his forehead. Like the one he has today.

The cloud is now a chubby girl with a shock of dark hair and a little pigtail sticking out from behind her head.

His deepest desire is to have a baby girl of his own—to cuddle, to pamper, to love unconditionally. More than anything else, he wants to raise a girl into womanhood. His lips quiver in the semblance of a smile as he thinks of when his fiancée told him that she too wanted a baby girl first. Their plan was to have half-a-dozen children born of love for each other, but the first has to be a girl.

The cloud sheds her clothes with bewitching slowness, revealing enticing curves, clefts and shadows. Suraj feels an unexpected stirring between his legs, shocking him. At this moment? Stretched out on hard pavement stones, bleeding to death?

But all that love around him will go waste. He knows it. He is not going to feel Papa's rough hands thump him on his back anymore. Nor will he feel the soft, clinging hug of Mummy's arms. Big brother is thousands of miles away in Australia. How can he be here to ruffle Suraj's hair with his surgeon's bony fingers and his lopsided smile?

And *her*? Suraj is never going to touch that alluring softness that she has wickedly kept off-limits till their marriage. Not even a kiss! He will never gaze into the crystal of endless possibilities in her sparkling, brown eyes; hear the music of her voice; smell her sweetness or make ...

An adorable baby girl.

98

Allah never said the road would be easy. But He said, *I will be with those who have patience.*

Khalid holds the bottle sticking out of his belly and gives a gentle tug. He suppresses the urge to scream and beg for mercy. There is no one to hear him. He leans against the wall and closes his eyes, waiting with patience for Allah's mercy.

And if My servants ask you about Me—behold, I am near; I respond to the call of he who calls, whenever he calls unto Me. Let them, then, respond unto Me, and believe in Me, so that they might follow the right way.

It is not actually true that there is no one to hear him. Allah has always heard him. When he was a little boy, wandering the streets, scavenging for food, a man of Allah—Haji Sa'ab—had taken him in, fed him, trained him to become an auto mechanic and before dying, bequeathed the garage to him. Is this not a message from Allah that he looks after those who look for Him?

This is my straight path, so follow it, and follow not diverse paths, lest they scatter you from its road.

No, the road has never been easy for a street orphan. It led him to the path of crime and delinquency. Still so young, Khalid had become angry and scared and frustrated. But now he knows that before getting frustrated, one must remember that one never knows where Allah has placed goodness. Allah manifested in the form of the wonderful human being, Haji Sa'ab, who guided him back to the straight path. Khalid has kept to that path.

One who works is the friend of Allah, and one who does not work is considered by Allah to be His enemy.

He has worked hard. From the rudimentary tin shed he inherited, he developed the garage into a proper service centre for two-wheelers with facilities for fitting accessories and doing paintwork. From just two employees, the garage now has seven, including an accountant. The money coming in isn't bad either.

The charity of those who expend their wealth in the Way of Allah may be likened to a grain of corn, which produces seven ears and each ear yields a hundred grains.

He has not kept all the bounty of the Almighty to himself but has shared it with generosity. He has helped his employees in their times of need, he has donated to charities and never shied away from offering shelter to the homeless or food to the hungry. That is how that poor girl, Fatima, delivered her babies in the garage. Yes, at least there is satisfaction that Khalid has used his money in the way of Allah.

Man is created weak ... Every son of Adam commits mistakes and the best of the wrongdoers are those who repent.

Alas, there have been weaknesses and mistakes. He has succumbed to temptations of the flesh when he should have cast his eyes down and fasted instead. Flesh is weak indeed. He yearns to be loved. And because he hasn't found it yet, he buys it every now and then. But he has never forced himself upon anyone. He pays for all labour of love.

He truly repents his transgressions. He repents not getting married and starting a family to produce more children of Allah. He repents indulging in violence which was not always in the cause of Allah. He repents not doing enough good deeds that will ensure his entry into the haloed Garden after death.

The Angel of Death who is charged with taking your souls will take your souls; then you will be returned to your Lord.

It is time, then. Khalid caresses the slimy glass of the bottle draining his life force. Maybe his last deed will count for something while he awaits the Day of Judgement in Barzakh. Angels Munkar and Nakir will consider how he gave up his life trying to protect two innocent children from the sons of Shaitan. Yes, he is ready to be returned to his Lord.

La ilaha il-lallah. Allah hu akbar.

There is only one God, and that is Allah. Allah is Almighty.

Allahumma, Ighfir li.

O Allah! Forgive me.

99

So, this is what a battlefield looks like—aflame, besmirched with blood, strewn with bodies, shrouded in smoke, drowned in cries of pain and bloodcurdling howls of hate. A wasteland.

Who would have thought that this morning, when he tied his turban, that he was dressing up for his first war? It was to be a day for love, friendship, hope and celebration with the love of his life, Thoi, and his oldest friends. Not for apocalypse.

When he took the oath to defend the nation, he believed he would be protecting it from the enemy on the outside. When his course mates looked forward to deployment, it was against those enemies. They hoped for glory in battlefields at the borders. Not on familiar streets and in the marketplaces they had grown up in. Not against a horde of their own countrymen destroyed by hatred.

Their countrymen, ignorant and proud and pious and narrow-minded, flooding the streets with venom from their hearts. Who hurl discordance and disharmony at each other, swamping reason. Who stake their claim with colours of fluttering cloth and marks on their foreheads. Who grade people by the colour of their skin, the texture of their hair or the shapes of their noses or eyes. Who think land can be divided by lines drawn on a piece of paper and a bird from one side of a line cannot sit on the branch of a tree on the other side. Who are so satiated and ensconced in plenty that they consider meagreness a crime. Who romp in metallic splendour and crush dusty penury under giant wheels of galvanized rubber. Who feed on misery and get bloated on usury and oppression, flaunting layers of accoutrement over raw exposure to misfortunes. Who believe differences in anatomy allow them the licence to invade and penetrate other beings, forgetting their own genesis. Who equate phallic mechanics with a divine mandate to torture, mutilate and kill. Who shrink to wriggling nothingness when challenged with courage born out of righteous indignation. Who think a uniform given by we, the people, entitles them to pouring lead into those very people, down a barrel that can any day be turned and used to reverse the flow of power. Who slash, burn and maul their own as if one can still survive after gouging out one's own eyes, stabbing one's own heart or ripping open one's own belly. Who confuse one with a billion. Who don't understand that four different colours on the same swath of cloth are meant to be a symbol of oneness.

Angad pulls himself back from the edge of darkness. He thinks he can hear a small whimper from inside the shuttered shop he is guarding. He senses someone approaching him. He cannot do anything but will give every ounce of his failing strength to defend the entrance. Whoever is coming can only reach the little girl and her brother over his dead body. He braces himself and prays:

Deh Shiva bar mohey.

God, grant me this boon—that I never shy from righteous acts; that I fight without fear all foes in the battles of life; that

I claim victory with grit and determination; that Your glory be ingrained in my mind forever; that my highest deed be singing Your praises; that when my end comes I die fighting with limitless courage.
  Bole So Nihal, Sat Sri Akal!

100

'Ammi?'

Murad looks at Nafisa with big, round eyes. The angry screams of people have faded. There is an eerie silence that somehow makes him more uncomfortable. He clutches Nafisa's fingers in his tiny hand.

Nafisa shudders and draws her brother closer. She pulls back into a corner, hoping to become invisible. She makes Murad sit down cross-legged and settles next to him. She knows grown-ups cannot look down too much.

All they have to do is wait. Ammi will come for them soon. The big man with the red turban had said he would keep them safe till then. She believes him because his eyes are clear. Not dirty like those of that fat shopkeeper who always troubles Ammi. Nor simmering like the policeman's, the one who always scolds Ammi.

The smell floating in from outside is odd. She wrinkles her nose. Murad has no sense of smell. He can even smile at her with his foolish mouth that only has six teeth yet. He really is insufferable. Ammi says Nafisa was like him when she was little but Nafisa knows Ammi says it teasingly. No human being can be as stupid, useless or ugly as Murad. But how can she resist when he leans over and buries his head in her tummy? It does something—brings out a strange, protective instinct. A feeling similar to what she experiences when she sees a kitten or a puppy. She sighs and places her arms around her brother's head.

Why has the big, bearded man not come back with Ammi? Did he forget where he left them? That thought makes Nafisa frown. Grown-ups are so forgetful. They are forever promising things and then forgetting them They forget they have yelled at you and soon after, want a hug or a kiss. That is not fair. They also fight so much over such meaningless things and then they laugh if she fights with Murad over something as important as who will kiss Ammi first.

Will anyone remember where she and Murad had been left? This place is so unfamiliar. Should she go out and look for Ammi? It has been so quiet for so long. She could have eaten many ice creams in this much time.

'Ammi?' Murad asks, getting querulous.

'Ssshh!' Nafisa puts a finger on her lips and pinches Murad's arm with an angry glare. Murad starts to sob.

Remorse and guilt overcome Nafisa, and she tries to calm her brother down with a hug. He pushes her away and slaps her arm. She hits him back in admonishment, but hugs him in the next moment. Nafisa starts crying softly too.

EPILOGUE

Katya leaned against a wall and retched. A thick swirl of greasy smoke blew past, making her cough and gasp some more.

Joyo lowered his Canon XF300 camcorder and looked away from his colleague, shuffling his weight from one foot to the other. Beads of cold sweat formed on his forehead as he clenched his teeth, listening to Katya gag and splutter behind him. Hooking a podgy thumb through the grip, he pulled out a handkerchief and struggled to tie it across his smooth, pale face.

Turning back, he saw Katya cover her nose and mouth with her hand, her slim shoulders heaving. With a despondent sigh, Joyo offered his handkerchief to her. She accepted it with a grateful nod.

'You sure?' she asked.

'Your shirt's plain white.' Joyo nodded with a shrug.

Katya pulled out a water bottle from her sling bag and took a few nervous gulps.

Digging into his many-pocketed vest, Joyo fished out a pack of cigarettes. Casting a tired glance around, he selected a stick. He lit up and took a couple of deep puffs, letting out thick, sweet-smelling smoke.

'What?' Katya whispered, rolling her eyes. 'Joyo, everything is still smouldering. It's dangerous to light up. Put it out please.'

Joyo shrugged and jabbed a finger towards the burning vehicle across the street. Katya glared at her cameraman and tied the handkerchief across her nose like a mask. Her light brown curls were moist with sweat as she ran her fingers through them and tied a loose knot.

Joyo puffed rapidly and threw away the stub. He shook his head like a wet dog and grinned with satisfaction.

The smoke had cleared a little and the charred wreckage of a toppled PCR van was now visible, lying in a pool of smouldering oil. Angry clouds of steam and black smoke billowed out from the vehicle as two firemen hosed it down with water from a tanker parked across the street. Short tongues of orange flame still flickered inside. The firemen directed the water away from the window to the burning tyres. Katya recoiled and tapped Joyo on his shoulders, pointing at the steaming window frame. Joyo shouldered his camcorder and trained his lens on it.

Katya peered at the display as Joyo zoomed in. A skeletal arm protruded from the opening: blackened flesh, mostly burned away, palm facing upwards and fingers slightly curled, as if begging for mercy. Wincing, Katya turned away.

The police van was not the only vehicle burning. As they walked down the street, they passed dozens of battered, overturned and burning vehicles. Katya stopped near a black SUV parked at an angle to the opposite pavement, next to a badly burnt ice cream cart with a singed sign that had once read 'Zinga Ice Cream'. The smoke-blackened chassis of two autorickshaws stood at the curb. The SUV's roof had caved in, the hood and doors were heavily pockmarked and dented and every one of its glass surfaces was shattered.

The passenger door in the rear left was ajar. A pair of naked, lifeless legs dangled out. It had bruises and deep gashes along the thighs. From where she stood, Katya could see a glimpse of a tattered fuchsia fabric that could have once been a skirt.

Joyo kept shooting as Katya slowly made her way along the pavement, avoiding battered or charred bodies and stumbling on rocks, bricks and broken bottles. She made a strange picture in Joyo's frame: a solitary angel in denim jeans and a white shirt walking through hell.

A melee of policemen, firefighters and paramedics ran helter-skelter, shouting and cursing. A young policeman halted Katya and asked her to turn back. She flashed her special-access crime-scene pass. Just as the policeman started to argue, they heard a shout from a fireman—pointing frantically at the overturned ice cream cart. The policeman waved Katya on before running towards the mangled cart. Policemen and firemen swooped in on the spot.

'Want to go over?' Joyo asked, his brows furrowed.

'Let things settle down there,' Katya said, walking on. 'If someone is alive near the cart, we can try to interview him … or her … when they take them to the first-aid centre.' She gestured towards the row of ambulances parked in an open plaza in the main shopping area.

She looked around. It was a commercial area, with offices, eateries and shops. The main street running past the market was intersected by narrow lanes that branched out on either side. Several shops were still burning, as were some cars. Scattered groups of firemen manoeuvred their hoses in an attempt to douse the flames and rescue teams scampered about to clear the street of the dead and injured. It seemed there were just not enough personnel on the ground to deal with the chaos.

Katya's cell phone rang and she scooped it out of her sling bag. She checked the display and flashed it at Joyo, who wrinkled his nose.

'Yes, Auro?' Katya put the phone on speaker for Joyo's benefit.

'Are you there yet?' a high-pitched voice screeched out. Joyo hung his head in exasperation. 'I wasn't getting through to you.'

'Auro, it is a five-minute drive from office,' Katya said, pursing her lips. 'Of course, I am here. With Joyo. The cell phone service has just been restored it seems.'

'What happened?'

'Look, we heard of this riot just ...' Katya checked her watch, '...just about thirty minutes back and we have already been here for the past twenty. Seems even the police and fire brigade arrived only minutes before we did. We are the first reporters here.'

'So, what's your damn report?' Auro's whiny voice demanded.

'This—this place is a *war zone*,' Katya said, taking in the burning shops, the charred vehicles, the body bags being rushed to waiting vans and the crowd of injured assembled in the plaza.

'What is it that happened?' Auro asked again, her voice now shriller with urgency.

'*I don't bloody know yet!*' Katya shouted back, her cheekbones flushed and eyes flashing. 'I tried to ask a few policemen. They don't seem to know either. They are busy putting bodies in bags and helping the firemen and the medics. I asked a few survivors, but none of them have a clue. I told you ... the place is goddamn chaos.'

'Ask that fatso Joyo to upload some grabs,' Auro ordered. Joyo stuck up a middle finger at Katya's phone.

'We need to find a place to sit down,' Katya tried to sound calm. 'He needs to transfer the files to my laptop and then upload them on the cloud. And where the hell is the OB van?'

'Apparently no vehicles are being allowed into the area by the police,' Auro informed. 'You have to manage somehow for now. Send me some footage ASAP.'

'Fucking asshole,' Katya muttered and started walking ahead with Joyo following.

'What? Speak into the damn mouthpiece,' Auro screamed. 'Why is your voice so muffled?'

'Because,' Katya hissed, tearing off her mask. 'I have a fucking handkerchief tied across my face to keep the stench of burning corpses out. Understand?'

There was a moment of stunned silence.

'How many?' Auro finally asked. 'How many dead? Give me some numbers, facts, names, faces, footage. What the hell caused it? Communal? Political? Protest? Criminal? What? *Find out!* We have to be the first ones going on air with this.'

Katya stopped in her tracks and moved the phone away from her ear. Was that the faint sound of someone wailing? It sounded like a child crying. No ... children. Certainly more than one. Frantically, she looked around. They were in front of what looked like a garment shop. Three bodies were lying across its entrance, blocking it.

'Hang on, Auro,' Katya whispered into the phone. 'I need to check this out.'

The body propped up against the left jamb of the grilled door wore a pathan suit and had a crescent beard. His grimy taqiyah cap was tilted across his forehead, lending a macabre jauntiness to his young face. A broken beer bottle stuck out from his stomach. Drops of sticky blood were still falling from the mouth of the bottle. His tunic and the dust on the pavement were muddy brown with his blood.

The second man, in a black t-shirt, was sprawled face up on the pavement—diagonally blocking the entrance—the left half of his face bashed in with a brick that was lying next to his head, soaked in red. There was a smudged vermilion tilak on his forehead. His right hand was clenched tight around a bent curtain rod.

The third body was of a young man wearing a red tie and maroon turban. His once-pristine white shirt was drenched in blood. His beard and moustache, neatly trimmed, were caked in scarlet dirt. He was wedged in the entrance, both his hands still stuck in the bars of the collapsible gate grill, as if trying to prevent anyone from entering. His blood-splattered head hung lifeless on his chest. Katya gagged.

'What?' Auro hissed with impatience from Katya's phone. 'Talk to me, Katya!'

Ignoring Auro, Katya clicked on the camera of her phone. She took a step closer and stumbled. With a frown of confusion, she took another unsteady step and stopped. She held up her phone and tried to keep it steady but couldn't.

Her arm dipped and swayed as she struggled to maintain her balance. Taking a deep breath, she grabbed the phone with both her hands, pursed her lips and narrowed her eyes in concentration.

Framed in her display screen were the corpses of three men. The pavement in the foreground was strewn with bricks, broken bottles, abandoned footwear and was besmirched with dark red patches.

'Why the fuck are you not answering me, Katya?' Auro screeched.

Katya grimaced and recoiled from the phone.

'Where is that lead visual you promised?' Auro demanded. 'I've been waiting.'

'Uh … Joyo and I were hunting for something dramatic for you,' Katya said. 'We found nothing that will please you.'

'What does that mean?' Auro demanded. 'No dead bodies, no burnt vehicles or buildings? No wailing wounded?'

'Oh, there was enough of that,' Katya said, staring at the three bodies. 'And you want a story to run with the visuals, don't you?'

'Err, obviously! Did you speak to anyone at all?'

Katya glanced at Joyo who rolled his eyes and looked away.

'Uh,' Katya said. 'Different people … I … I was a bit … distracted with … with all this horrible mess here.'

'Did you record them?' Auro asked. 'Sound bites? Close-ups? The nation wants to know what happened!'

There was glum silence on the phone.

Katya gingerly stepped closer to the entrance and tried to peer inside. Joyo trained his camcorder on her, biting his lips to keep calm. They could now clearly hear the sounds of sobbing children from inside.

'Can you hear me?' Katya said aloud, clearing her throat.

'Of course, I can,' Auro barked back.

'I am Katya ... didi ... your big sister,' Katya called out, ignoring Auro.

'You wish!'

One of the voices fell silent. The other—of a toddler—continued bawling.

'Come out ... please,' Katya said softly. 'I am here to take care of you. Your Ma has sent me.'

'*What's going on?*' Auro's voice demanded. 'Whose Ma?'

Katya waited silently, her eyes focused on the entrance of the shop. She heard sounds of movement from inside and held her breath. An ambulance with its siren hooting sped past behind them and then it was suddenly quiet again.

A little girl of four or five holding a toddler barely half her size emerged from the darkness inside the shop. They were both in dirty, bloodstained rags. The girl halted behind the dead man lying across the entrance. She stared at Katya through a mop of filthy hair, empty eyes peering out of a hollow face.

'Where is Ammi?' she asked Katya.

'Ammi?' the toddler intoned.

Katya kept her eyes on the two children and brought her phone up to her ear.

'Joyo is shooting this, Auro,' she said into the phone. 'I am going to send you a pic from my phone. Open your damn broadcast with this image—it is worth a million words. I will go and talk to some survivors and piece together the full story. You will have your report soon.' She disconnected and switched to camera mode.

On the screen, she saw a turbaned, bearded youth seemingly protecting a blood-smeared girl of four or five carrying an even younger child in her arms with great effort. To the left was the body of a man wearing a grimy taqiyah cap with a bottle embedded in his gut. The third man, in a black t-shirt, with his head half smashed, was lying in the foreground.

Katya clicked. Changing the angle of her phone just a little she clicked a few more times. Going into her photo gallery, she reviewed her pics. She smiled in satisfaction and showed the best one to Joyo who gave her a thumbs up. Katya selected all and sent them to Auro.

'The grill seems to be locked,' she told Auro. 'Keep shooting. I will move the body away and try to pry it open. If I can't then you will need to help me out. They will edit later. I want you to get a visual of me bringing out these kids. Get it?'

'Got it,' Joyo said. 'Katya for Magsaysay Award—that's my motto.'

Katya glared at him and moved towards the body blocking the gate. She cocked her head and peered at the big man. It was going to be a task for her. His hands were stuck in the grill. She gave Joyo a worried look.

'The road to the Magsaysay is tough and lonely,' Joyo grimaced, making no effort to help Katya.

Leaning forward, she tried to pry away the man's left hand first. The little girl and boy had stopped sobbing and were looking at her with curiosity.

'Don't touch the children!' the turbaned man growled, snapping his head up and staring with savage, bloodshot eyes into her own.

Katya screamed and staggered back.

'Joyo! He is alive!'

ACKNOWLEDGEMENTS

In Book I of Aristotle's *Politiká*, he observes, 'Man is by nature a social animal.' That is why sociologists and psychologists study the collective behaviour of humans to understand them better. Social norms, morals, culture, politics and even macroeconomics are considered in the analysis of the aggregative behaviour of humans. Mob psychology is a stream of knowledge in itself. *Inside Burn* makes an effort to expose the anatomy of a riot by placing individuals and their actions under the lens of a literary microscope.

The thought of exploring the concept of 'spontaneous riots' came to me after reading several news articles that reported riots in different cities or places that didn't seem to have any single underlying or apparent cause. They were probably an accumulation of individual anger, frustrations, fears and reactions, and a result of several fissures and schisms in society. As I read more about such riots, I realized that such 'spontaneous riots' were seen across the globe and social scientists had been researching the phenomena for some time now. This book is inspired by many of those research papers, articles and books. I acknowledge their silent but important contribution to this piece of fiction.

Acknowledgements

As always, Shampa, my wife, was my first testing ground for the first draft I wrote. This time, I waited till I finished before handing over the manuscript to her. She is an avid and quick reader, but she took me by surprise when she told me a few hours later that she couldn't stop reading because of the breakneck pace and that she came out of the read feeling stunned and numbed. It was the most encouraging thing I could have heard, given the unusual theme and plot of the book and I thank her for that. Most of all, I thank her for enduring the days and weeks when I am cocooned in the world of my book as I write. It's not an easy task to deal with an author whose brain is on fire.

The very next day, I sent the manuscript off to my dear friend and literary agent, Priya Doraswamy of Lotus Lane Literary, who lives in the US. The immediate excitement and enthusiasm she expressed after reading it made me feel even more confident about the book. I have known Priya for nearly a decade now and I highly value her inputs, advice and efforts to bring my books to life. I am grateful for that.

I was delighted that HarperCollins India didn't take much time to accept the submission and express their eagerness to publish the book. Even more joyful for me was that Poulomi Chatterjee was to be my editor once again. I have worked with Poulomi before, and have always marvelled at the sensitive, incisive and intuitive editing she does. I am thankful for her hard work that has lent shine and polish to the original text.

I am also grateful to Shreya Mukherjee, who worked with patience and diligence on this book. We had a good vibe working together. I must express my appreciation to the design and art team of HarperCollins India for coming up with a bold, contemporary and aesthetic cover.

Last but not least, I thank my mother who ensured I cleared my exams despite my best efforts not to, and who was always extremely proud of my writing from my first 'stories' in primary school. She passed away while I was writing this book. She would have once again puffed up with maternal pride seeing this book in print. My prayers of thanks to you, Mummy.

A special shout out to 'Tavern' for their endurance and friendship. They know who they are!

BIBLIOGRAPHY & RELATED READING

Albanesius, C. (2010, October 26). Apple buying Sony? Probably not. *PC Magazine*. Retrieved from http://www.pcmag.com/article2/0,2817,2371467,2371400.asp.

Baier, Annette. 'Pilgrim's Progress: Review of David Gauthier, Morals by Agreement.' *Canadian Journal of Philosophy* Vol. 18, No. 2. (June 1988): 315–330.

Baier, Annette. 1994. *Moral Prejudices: Essays on Ethics*. Cambridge: Harvard University Press.

Blumer, H. (1969). Collective behavior. In A.M. Lee (Ed.), *Principles of Sociology* (pp. 165–221). New York, NY: Barnes and Noble.

Braybrooke, David. 1976. 'The Insoluble Problem of the Social Contract.' *Dialogue* Vol. XV, No. 1: 3–37.

Buford, B. (1991) *Among the Thugs: The Experience, and the Seduction, of Crowd Violence*. New York: W.W. Norton & Co.

David D. Haddock & Daniel D. Polsby Why Riots Happen: Spontaneous (Dis)order: The Incentives and Entrepreneurs of Mass Crime. https://fee.org/articles/why-riots-happen/

DiStefano, Christine. 1991. *Configurations of Masculinity: A Feminist Perspective on Modern Political Theory*. Ithaca, NY: Cornell University Press.

Dowlut, R. (1983) 'The Right to Arms: Does the Constitution or the Predilection of Judges Reign?' *Oklahoma Law Review* 36(1): 65—105.

Downes, B.T. (1968). 'The social characteristics of riot cities: A comparative study'. *Social Science Quarterly, 49*, 504–520.

Feldberg, M. (1980). *The Turbulent Era: Riot and Disorder in Jacksonian America*. New York, NY: Oxford University Press.

Filmer, Robert. *'Patriarcha' and Other Writings*. Cambridge University Press (1991).

Gauthier, David. 1986. *Morals by Agreement*. Oxford: Oxford University Press.

Gauthier, David. 1988. 'Hobbes's Social Contract.' *Noûs* 22: 71–82.

Gauthier, David. 1990. *Moral Dealing: Contract, Ethics, and Reason*. Cornell: Cornell University Press.

Gauthier, David. 1991. 'Why Contractarianism?' in Vallentyne 1991: 13–30.

Gilligan, Carol. 1982. *In a Different Voice: Psychological Theory and Women's Development*. Cambridge: Harvard University Press.

Ginsberg, Allen. 'Howl'. https://www.poetryfoundation.org/poems/49303/howl

Goode, E. & Ben-Yehuda, N. (2009). *Moral Panics: The Social Construction of Deviance*. Malden, MA: Wiley-Blackwell.

Goode, E. (1992). *Collective behavior*. Fort Worth, TX: Harcourt Brace Jovanovich.

Gurr, T.R. (1989). Protest and rebellion in the 1960s: The United States in world perspective. In T.R. Gurr (Ed.), *Violence in America: Protest, Rebellion, Reform* (Vol. 2, pp. 101–130). Newbury Park, CA: Sage.

Hampton, Jean. 1986. *Hobbes and the Social Contract Tradition*. Cambridge: Cambridge University Press.

Hampton, Jean. 1993. 'Feminist Contractarianism.' In Antony, Louise M. and Witt, Charlotte (Eds). 1993. *A Mind of One's Own: Essays on Reason and Objectivity.* Boulder CO: Westview Press, Inc.: 1993: 227–255.

Held, Virginia. 1977. 'Rationality and Reasonable Cooperation.' *Social Research* (Winter 1977): 708–744.

Held, Virginia. 1993. *Feminist Morality: Transforming Culture, Society, and Politics.* Chicago: The University of Chicago Press.

Hobbes, Thomas. 1651. *Leviathan.* C.B Macpherson (Ed.). London: Penguin Books (1985)

Kavka, Gregory S. 1986. *Hobbesian Moral and Political Theory.* Princeton: Princeton University Press.

Locke, John. *Two Treatises of Government and A Letter Concerning Toleration.* Yale University Press (2003).

Macpherson, C.B. 1973. *Democratic Theory: Essays in Retrieval.* Oxford: Clarendon Press.

McPhail, C. & Wohlstein, R.T. (1983). Individual and collective behaviors within gatherings, demonstrations, and riots. *Annual Review of Sociology, 9,* 579–600.

McPhail, C. (1971). 'Civil disorder participation: A critical examination of recent research'. *American Sociological Review, 36,* pp. 1058–1073.

Miller, D.L. (2000). *Introduction to Collective Behavior and Collective Action* (2nd ed.). Springfield, IL: Waveland Press.

Mills, Charles. 1997. *The Racial Contract.* Cornell University Press.

Nozick, Robert. 1974. *Anarchy, State and Utopia.* New York: Basic Books.

Oberschall, A. (1967). 'The Los Angeles riot of August 1965'. *Social Problems, 15,* 322–341.

Okin, Susan Moller. 1989. *Justice, Gender, and the Family.* New York: Basic Books.

Pateman, Carole. 1988. *The Sexual Contract*. Stanford: Stanford University Press.

Plato. *Five Dialogues*. (Trans. G.M.A. Grube) Hackett Publishing Company (1981).

Plato. *Republic*. (Trans. G.M.A. Grube, Revised by C.D.C. Reeve) Hackett Publishing Company (1992).

Poundstone, William. 1992. *Prisoner's Dilemma: John Von Neumann, Game Theory, and the Puzzle of the Bomb*. New York: Doubleday.

Rawls, John. 1971. *A Theory of Justice*. Harvard University Press.

Rawls, John. 1993. *Political Liberalism*. Columbia University Press.

Rosenfeld, M.J. (1997). Celebration, Politics, Selective Looting and Riots: A Micro Level Study of the Bulls Riot of 1992 in Chicago. *Social Problems, 44,* 483–502.

Rousseau, Jean-Jacques. *The Basic Political Writings*. (Trans. Donald A. Cress) Hackett Publishing Company (1987).

Rubenstein, R.E. (1970). *Rebels in Eden: Mass Political Violence in the United States*. Boston, MA: Little, Brown.

Rule, J.B. (1988). *Theories of Civil Violence*. Berkeley: University of California Press.

Sandel, Michael. 1982. *Liberalism and the Limits of Justice*. Cambridge: Cambridge University Press.

Schelling, T.C. (1960) *The Strategy of Conflict*. Cambridge: Harvard University Press.

Types of Collective Behaviour. http://open.lib.umn.edu/sociology/chapter/21-1-types-of-collective-behavior/

Vallentyne, Peter (Ed.) 1991. *Contractarianism and Rational Choice: Essays on David Gauthier's Morals by Agreement*. New York: Cambridge University Press.

Waskow, A.I. (1967). *From Race Riot to Sit-in: 1919 and the 1960s*. Garden City, NY: Anchor Books.

What Causes Riots. https://whistlinginthewind.org/2013/02/28/what-causes-riots/

ABOUT THE AUTHOR

Sanjay Bahadur is the director general of Income Tax Investigation for Telangana, Andhra Pradesh and Odisha, posted in Hyderabad. He has an MA in economics from University of Bombay, an MBA from University of Birmingham, UK, and has completed courses from IIM Bangalore and Syracuse University, USA. Apart from being a prolific writer, he is also an avid cyclist, holds a black belt in both karate and taekwondo and promotes learning self-defence for girls and women.

His debut novel, *The Sound of Water*, was longlisted for the inaugural Man Asian Literary Prize 2007 and earned international critical acclaim. His subsequent novels, *Hul: Cry Rebel* (2013) and *Bite of the Black Dogs* (2017) gained critical acclaim and glowing reviews, with the latter being optioned for a feature film. *Inside Burn* is his fourth novel.

HarperCollins *Publishers* India

At HarperCollins India, we believe in telling the best stories and finding the widest readership for our books in every format possible. We started publishing in 1992; a great deal has changed since then, but what has remained constant is the passion with which our authors write their books, the love with which readers receive them, and the sheer joy and excitement that we as publishers feel in being a part of the publishing process.

Over the years, we've had the pleasure of publishing some of the finest writing from the subcontinent and around the world, including several award-winning titles and some of the biggest bestsellers in India's publishing history. But nothing has meant more to us than the fact that millions of people have read the books we published, and that somewhere, a book of ours might have made a difference.

As we look to the future, we go back to that one word—a word which has been a driving force for us all these years.

Read.